D0397674

Parade
of
Shadows

Also by Gloria Whelan

HOMELESS BIRD
LISTENING FOR LIONS
SUMMER OF THE WAR
CHU JU'S HOUSE

ANGEL ON THE SQUARE
THE IMPOSSIBLE JOURNEY
BURYING THE SUN
THE TURNING

FRUITLANDS
MIRANDA'S LAST STAND
INDIAN SCHOOL

ONCE ON THIS ISLAND
FAREWELL TO THE ISLAND
RETURN TO THE ISLAND

Parade
of
Shadows

GLORIA WHELAN

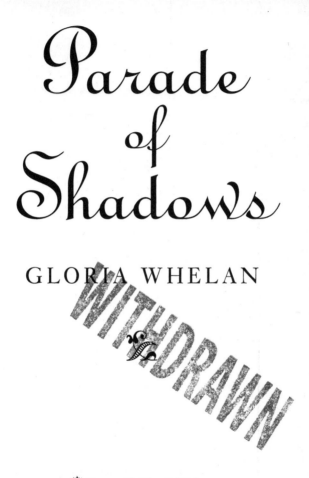

HarperCollins*Publishers*

www.harpercollinschildrens.com
Library of Congress Cataloging-in-Publication Data
Whelan, Gloria.
    Parade of shadows / Gloria Whelan. — 1st ed.
       p.   cm.
    Summary: In 1907, sixteen-year-old Julia Hamilton, happy to accom-
pany her diplomat father on a tour of the Ottoman-controlled cities of
Istanbul, Damascus, Palmyra, and Aleppo, soon finds the journey increasingly
hazardous as she begins to uncover her father's true mission and the secret
motivations of the other travelers in their group.
    ISBN: 978-0-06-089028-5 (trade)
    ISBN: 978-0-06-089029-2 (lib. bdg.)
    [1. Voyages and travels—Fiction. 2. Fathers and daughters—Fiction.
3. Spies—Fiction. 4. Turkey—History—Ottoman Empire, 1288–1918—
Fiction. 5. Middle East—History—20th century—Fiction.] I. Title.
PZ7.W5718Par 2007   2006103477
[Fic]—dc22   CIP
                                                              AC

            Typography by Larissa Lawrynenko
             1 3 5 7 9 10 8 6 4 2
                  ❖ First Edition

to

Mary Beth Smith

I

DURHAM PLACE

THE LETTER WAS addressed to my father, but I read it over and over. It was my escape, my magic carpet, a charm conjured up to deliver me from sixteen years of dull custody.

> *Charles Watson & Sons*
> *Travel Agents*
> *114 Piccadilly*
> *London, England*
> *March 14, 1907*

Mr. Carlton Hamilton
Durham Place
London, England

Dear Sir:

> *Herewith the details of your itinerary.*
> *You and your daughter, Miss Julia Hamilton, will*

travel by the Simplon Orient Express to Istanbul and thence by steamer to Beirut and from Beirut by rail to Damascus, where you will join our Syrian tour on April 2. The day of April 3 will be spent viewing the sights of Damascus under the direction of an experienced tour leader. On April 4 the tour will leave Damascus by dragoman, with overnight stops to include Jerud and Karyatein. There will be a four-day stay in Palmyra and thence by way of Forklus to Homs. From Homs the tour will travel to Aleppo and then again by dragoman to Ain el Beida and Antioch and thence by carriage to Alexandretta, where you will board your steamer.

In making these arrangements, the Messrs. Watson have endeavored to follow your wish "to view the classical ruins." I respectfully remind you that living quarters on much of the trip will consist of tents. Travel will be by horse. Since you will be traveling with your young daughter, we caution you that the trip will be rigorous, with little in the way of usual comforts. Should you wish for a more convenient route, we will be happy to accommodate you.

While we don't anticipate any unpleasantness, I feel you should be aware that this itinerary, like all travel through Syria, will be reviewed by the Turkish tourist office. I am sending under separate cover papers that you

will need to complete for your teskerés, *or Turkish*
passports.

Faithfully yours,
Edgar Reece

"Istanbul, Damascus, Palmyra, and Alexandretta." I said
the names over and over. Father and I would travel across
Europe, to Turkey and the Mediterranean Sea and even farther than my imagination could carry me. I traced our route
on the globe, the little round world that stood on a table in
my father's study. In the past the globe had been nothing
more than a geography lesson; now it was a promise.

On our journey I would be under my father's watchful
eye, and therefore I would not be entirely free; still, I hoped
that in distant countries my father's rules might be less
strict, so his presence wouldn't entirely spoil my determination to experience, for a change, a little life.

A chilly fog from the nearby Thames River nuzzled the
windows. As usual, I was feeling lost among the austere
Gothic chairs and forbidding Victorian portraits that ringed
the room like spies to catch me out. Our house on Durham
Place had always been too large for just Father and me. The
closed-off rooms gave the feeling that half the household
must be away. My father complained of coal bills and of

plumbing that disappointed daily, but we stayed on. I caught Father looking about the rooms as though, could he just stay long enough in the house, he would banish some unhappy memory. I knew that unhappy memory was of my mother's illness and death, a memory that colored everything in the house the darkest gray. As far as I myself was concerned, I often felt that my father didn't see me at all.

My own memories of my mother were of a pale face in a dark room. I remembered Mother's smiles as always welcoming but always sad, as if she believed each visit with me might turn out to be her last. If my mother was having a good day, I was sometimes allowed to gently brush the long, rippling waves of hair that fell to her waist. Even now, after all these years, I can smell its musty fragrance like damp leaves in a fall forest. I was six years old when Mother died.

Because he was assigned to the Arab Desk in England's Foreign Office, my father's world has always been wide. He was frequently off to Egypt or Morocco or the Red Sea, assisting England to get or trade or give away bits of land and sometimes whole countries. As a child I used to have an image of the inhabitants of a country waking up to find my father had acquired them like a new pocket watch or an interesting book. Even in my wildest dreams I had not believed I would someday have a glimpse of that world.

The idea for my accompanying Father on his trip had come about one evening when I stopped in his study to say good night. My relationship with my father was orderly. When he was in London, we bid each other good morning at breakfast, after which Father left for the Foreign Office and I went off to my classes at Miss Mumford's. On the infrequent nights when Father was not dining at his club, we dined together at home and he quizzed me on what I had learned that day at school. It was at one of these dinners that Father had told me that within the month he would be traveling to the Levant. The word *Levant*, he explained, meant the lands around the distant Mediterranean with exotic names like Syria and Jerusalem.

After dinner I went to his study and impulsively begged to be taken along. I couldn't bear the thought of remaining alone in the cheerless house one more time. It would be Easter vacation, so I would not even have my dreary classes of German composition and French conversation to occupy me. All the servants would be nesting cozily downstairs, and the great empty house would close in and suffocate me.

With obvious impatience to get back to work, Father stuck his pen into the thick file he had been reading and said, "It's not a suitable trip for you, Julia. I'm going to be trekking through the wastelands of Syria. You don't want to give up a perfectly comfortable home for that."

"I have nothing to do here." I pleaded with him.

Father frowned. "I hope you don't intend to cultivate the affectation of boredom. You are old enough to have your own interests." As an example to me of industriousness, he opened his file again.

Instead of slinking away as I usually did when confronted with Father's censure, I surprised myself by settling courageously down into a chair. I was wearing a silk dress, and the cool leather chilled my back and thighs. "You aren't bored, Father, because you always have interesting things to do," I said. I set my lips into two thin lines, something I have done since childhood on the rare occasions when I mean to have my way.

"This trip will entail inconvenience and discomfort, Julia, and has everything to do with duty and nothing to do with choice or pleasure. You'll be much happier here. You have your friends, and within proper limits you can go about as you please. Even during the months she was confined to her bed, I don't believe I ever heard your mother complain of having nothing to do."

I looked stricken and Father took a kinder tone. "I am sure it has not been easy for you rattling about here with a father who is often absent, but this is to be a rather short trip, and there is the added inconvenience of not knowing just what I will find. Officially I won't be traveling under the banner of the Foreign Office, so I must make do with haphazard accommodations."

"It sounds very mysterious," I said. Joseph Conrad's *The Secret Agent* had just come out, and I had been reading it with fascination, regretting that I had hardly any secrets, a state that seemed sad and dull to me.

"I'm afraid you are a romantic, Julia, an affliction you ought to suppress. There is no meeting ground between romanticism and reality. Romanticism is a state that invariably leads to dissatisfaction and disappointment and, I might add, boredom."

Father always got the better of me and, even more irksome, was usually right. I knew I was a romantic; everything seemed to me either worse or better than it was. "That's not entirely fair, Father. If I use my imagination, it's because I'm trying to make life more interesting."

"Life should be useful, not interesting. If you can't find any worthwhile charitable work and if your studies don't occupy you, you might try reading to improve your mind."

"Every time I bring up something that I have read, you dispute it and tell me the world isn't to be understood by reading books." This was what my father did, and I didn't see why I shouldn't say it.

"Ah, you have me there."

He seemed genuinely amused, and I was pleased to see him smile, something he seldom did. Father was in his early fifties, not tall but sturdily built, with sandy hair rapidly going gray and carefully trained against a natural wave. He had pale blue eyes concealed behind thick glasses. When he removed his glasses, his eyes appeared naked and gave his otherwise stern face a defenseless look. He took his glasses off now to polish them and also to gain time. "Well," he said, "I'll think it over. It might not be a bad thing to have you along.

"As I hope you know from your lessons, Julia, the Turkish sultan, Abdülhamid II, rules the Ottoman Empire, which stretches from the Arabian Peninsula north through Jerusalem and Syria to Armenia; westward into Europe across northern Greece, Albania, and Bosnia and Herzegovina; and out over the Mediterranean to Tripoli. The sultan, who is sometimes known as Abdul the Damned, has dismissed his parliament, inflicted grinding taxes, silenced the press, and, with the help of his spies, dispatched his critics in a number of unpleasant, even violent ways."

"Violent ways!" For once Father's history lesson was not boring, as I hoped soon to be traveling through the countries of Abdul the Damned. Perhaps I would even get to see some of the violent ways—from a safe distance, of course.

Father's lesson became even more interesting. "Just now, visitors are not allowed into Syria unless they take a tour overseen by a guide supplied by the sultan's Turkish government. The sultan is worried about the revolutionary Young Turks, who want to get rid of him and set up some sort of constitutional government. As unsettled as all this sounds, I believe the country is relatively safe. You would be able to sketch ruins from the real thing instead of having to run off to the British Museum to find them. Let me bring up the idea of your accompanying me with the Foreign Office." At that he began to study the file on his desk like a hungry man with a menu. I saw I was dismissed.

I hurried to my room, carrying all of Father's words with me as if they were some rare and delicious food to feed upon. He had said we would not know what we would find. So there would be surprises, perhaps even dangerous ones. I was excited by the prospect of change and thrilled at the idea of distant places. Of course, I would be very much in my father's company. In the house I could easily escape his scrutiny by slipping off to attend to something. Father believed girls had an endless reserve of foolish occupations. But I was sure that on the trip I would have some time for myself, time to form impressions for myself; for when I was with Father, I seemed unable to have my own ideas: His were strong enough for the both of us.

I had a streak of obstinacy, probably from my father, and I speculated upon what would happen if some demand made by my father, or a limitation imposed by him, reached that place in me where I would not give in. Which of us would win?

I put the question out of my head and thought only of the exciting adventures ahead of me. Surely Father would have his own matters to attend to; and I had my pastime of sketching, something that would give me the excuse I needed for a little time for myself, for there would be all kinds of wonders to sketch. Miss Mumford liked to have parents believe that her school brought out some special talent in their child. She had decided that my talent was to be drawing. In Miss Mumford's report to Father she had written, "Julia shows an ability for drawing, which we are encouraging." Since Father did not take the time to look at my work, he believed the report.

I knew what an artist was, and I knew I wasn't one. I told myself that I hadn't the ability to look at a thing and see what no one else can see, and then to make plain to everyone my discovery. Still, with all the fascinating sights before me, perhaps I would do better. Anyhow, if my father believed my drawings were a reason to allow my adventure, I would cheerfully wear down any number of pencils.

"Istanbul, Damascus, Palmyra, and Alexandretta." I said the words over again. They were the charm that would at last open the door of our gloomy house.

II

WARNING

W HEN THE NEXT day Father announced to me that I might go with him, he warned, "This will not be a trip to the perfumed sands of Arabia. Syria is hot and dusty, and most of the time we will be traveling by horse and living in tents." When he saw the pleasure on my face, he said, "Ah, I can see by your expression you are thinking you will be pursued by Arab princes on white steeds. Be disabused. British women who show their faces and bare their arms and legs are repugnant to Arab men. I must also warn you that though you may not be aware of it, danger will lie all about us. The Levant is treacherous territory. You are not to venture anywhere on your own."

So Father did mean for me to be under his close supervision. I didn't flatter myself that my father was anxious for my company on the trip—over the years there had been too little evidence of that. I guessed, instead, that he had come to the conclusion that my presence on this trip might in some mysterious way be an advantage to him. If that was so, what a lucky thing it was, for it was making it possible for me to have an adventure I could not have conjured up in my wildest dreams.

As the day of our departure drew near, my uncle Edgar and aunt Harriet invited us for a little farewell dinner. As Father and I passed through Berkeley Square, I studied the fat buds on the plane trees and the early tulips bright against the dark earth, wondering what flowers grew in Syria's sandy soil. All my thoughts now were for what was ahead of me. I lived in the present only by habit.

My uncle Edgar and aunt Harriet resided on South Audley Street. As Father and I entered the comfortable town house, I brightened at seeing my cousin Teddy down from Oxford. Teddy, though four years older than I was, treated me as a contemporary rather than a child, inviting me into his games of irritating adults.

Aunt Harriet hurried the men through their sherry. "I've had a special dinner cooked for you, a nice joint of beef. You won't get that on your travels. Cows are sacred there, aren't they?"

"That's India, Harriet," Father said, smiling. "It's pork you don't get in a Muslim country."

Teddy said, "I've got a friend, Lawrence, at Oxford, who would give anything to be going with you. He's even learning the Arab lingo. You speak it, don't you, Uncle Carlton?"

"Yes, just a bit now and then. They like it when you can answer them in their own language." I looked at my father but said nothing of my surprise. When I was very young, I had seen him studying a sheaf of papers and had crept up to his desk and peeked over his shoulder to see pages of dots and curves. My father had been amused at my puzzlement. "Arabic," he had explained, "like 'Ali Baba and the Forty Thieves.'" With no hesitation he had read off a page for me. I wondered why he was now denying that knowledge.

Uncle Edgar carved the roast, one juicy slab after another. "You must be mad even to consider taking Julia to a primitive country," he said, "with nothing but a heap of sand for a bed and boiled sheeps' eyes for dinner. That's all very well for you—it's your business; but I wonder at your dragging Julia along."

"Julia wants to find an Arab prince to marry," Teddy teased me.

"Be serious, Teddy," Uncle Edgar said. "There are some very frightening uprisings and wars going on in those countries. I understand the sultan is having trouble with his far-flung empire."

14

"Sultan Abdülhamid keeps rather a tight rein on every-one," Father said. "It makes his subjects a bit restless. The Greeks would like their land back, the Arabs thirst for independence, the Armenians are executed under the sultan, and the Jews want a homeland."

"We offered the Jews six thousand square miles in British East Africa," Uncle Edgar said. "Rather a handsome gift, I should think."

"Why would they want miles of remote Africa," Teddy asked, "when it has nothing to do with them?"

"Exactly the point they made," Father said. "But as long as Sultan Abdülhamid rules the Ottoman Empire, the Jews will never get a homeland."

While all this conversation about Greeks and Armenians and Jews was going on around me, I had let my mind wander to decisions about what I would pack and just how I would wash my hair in a country where water might be scarce. I was going in order to see distant lands and strange sights, not to be caught up in quarrels among people of whom I knew nothing.

Uncle Edgar, having done his duty by carving up the joint, signaled to the maid to pass along the fruits of his labor. "Do you allow this revolutionary Young Turk movement any credence? The Young Turks seem to turn up everywhere with their talk of restoring a constitutional government in Turkey. I don't suppose the Foreign Office can be too happy with a lot of rebels like that whipping up nationalism among the Armenians and Greeks and Arabs?"

Father appeared reluctant to answer the question. He held up his wineglass. "An excellent claret," he said.

At once my ears pricked up. You could tell as much from what Father didn't or wouldn't say as you could from what he did say. I suspected he was hiding something and was glad to guess that there might be secrets traveling with us.

Teddy also noticed Father's evasiveness. "I suppose England's Foreign Office has its own scheme for the Turkish Empire and is not anxious to deal with revolutionaries."

Father, who was fond of Teddy, now gave him a cold stare. "Not that I am aware, Teddy, but I am sure the Foreign Office would be glad to take your advice on the matter."

Teddy flushed and bent over his plate, stung by Father's rebuke, for he meant to be amusing, not malicious.

Always uncomfortable with disagreements, Aunt Harriet broke in. "I'm more annoyed than I can say. I've gone to no end of trouble to give you a good dinner and I've not heard one word of appreciation, only nasty quarrels about countries that can't possibly have anything to do with us."

Father regretted his show of temper. "You must share part of the blame, Harriet," he said, putting his hand over hers. "You spoil us by giving us such good dinners that we have learned to take them for granted, but you have outdone yourself this evening."

No further reference was made to the trip until we were leaving, when Father said, "By the way, Edgar, thank you for arranging the letter of credit for the trip with your bank."

"Pleased to do it. But doesn't the Foreign Office usually take care of those things for you?"

"This is to be a pleasure trip. My Foreign Office business ends in Beirut."

I said nothing. But if this was to be simply a pleasure trip, why had Father had to discuss with the Foreign Office my accompanying him? And when had Father ever done something for pleasure? I thought with a thrill that the trip was becoming more mysterious.

There were farewells with warm embraces all around. Teddy whispered in my ear, "I hope you learn belly dancing," and Aunt Harriet took me aside and also whispered in my ear, "I envy you your great adventure, Julia. I only wish I had seen more of the world. Will you write and tell me all about it?"

At Durham Place, as I started for the stairway, anxious

to do my last-minute packing, Father called me into his study. He took a cigar from a silver humidor and carefully clipped off the tip. Slowly he drew off the cigar's red-and-gold paper ring. When I was a child, he saved the paper rings for me and I paraded about with them on all ten fingers. In those days, I remember, before Mother's death, how jolly and amused Father had been by my childish whims.

After a careful lighting of his cigar Father said, "It is awkward to tell you this, Julia, for I know you will immediately jump to the most foolish conclusions, but for the purposes of the trip I am simply to be a solicitor on vacation. The Foreign Office is not to be mentioned. There is nothing deceitful in that. You know I read law before going into the government. I will be doing some looking and listening, and I can't be effective if I am associated with Britain's Foreign Office. What it comes down to is that, at the moment, the Turks don't altogether trust the British. In fact, the sultan is a bit rabid in his suspicions."

I caught my breath and felt my eyes grow large. Father must have noticed, for he quickly added, "None of that need concern you, Julia. This is to be regarded as a pleasure trip insofar as jogging about the desert can be called a pleasure. We are to present ourselves as looking at ruins—and we will see some quite impressive ones. Now, no questions. You will have plenty to do to get yourself in order."

The sense of danger I felt was pleasant, as if I had been given an exciting book to read. That I would be living in the book made it all the more interesting. As I mounted the stairway, I told myself that after the adventure of the trip, I was sure to be a different person. But what kind of person?

III

THE ORIENT EXPRESS

AN ESCORT OF SEAGULLS accompanied the boat train that carried us from England to the port of Calais in France. It seemed odd to be traveling over the water on a train, and even odder to look out the window in Calais and find all the signs in French. At the train station, when I saw the Simplon Orient Express with its sign, CALAIS–ISTANBUL, my excitement grew, for I would soon be on the train, and the name "Istanbul" reached farther than my imagination.

Father and I each had our own compartment on the Orient Express. I looked about at the comfortable couch that would be my bed, the shiny metal sink that neatly folded away, and most of all the window, where every second I was being carried farther and farther from home. At last, trying to be sociable, I tore myself from my little room to visit Father, who briefly looked up from his papers and said, "Don't feel you have to keep me company." I slunk back to my room a bit less pleased.

Later, when Father called for me on the way to the dining car, he was apologetic. "I didn't mean to send you off like that, but the trip is becoming something of a nuisance. The Foreign Office is rather unrealistic in what they expect."

So our mysterious trip *was* an official one. "What are they asking of you?" I thought the question was appropriate, and I longed to be taken into the place my father inhabited, a place of important affairs. Perhaps such knowledge would open a door for me into the real world.

Father's response was brisk. "Fortunately, that need not concern you." The door slammed shut.

Away from home, with no rules to fall back on, I felt uncertain and out of place beside my father, who appeared perfectly sure of himself, ordering in French and choosing a wine with conviction. I watched the waiter become respectful and helpful in proportion to the number of my father's demands. I, too, would have liked to occasionally make demands, but it wasn't in me. My instincts were to give the least trouble I could.

We had our dinner at the dining car's second sitting, so it was already dark. From the windows I watched the lights of the small French villages rush by like distant meteors. A couple at the table across the aisle from us leaned toward each other, their faces flushed from the rosy light of the pink-shaded lamps. Their food meant nothing to them; it was a distraction. I wondered if I would ever find someone to look at me the way that man looked at that woman. If this journey was taking me to a faraway place, would it take me that far?

Father followed my covert glance. "That kind of attachment may look very pretty, but it's not the kind of thing you build a life on. I wonder at their putting on that show in public." Father's voice was bitter. I supposed it was because with Mother gone, that part of his life was over, and I felt sorry for him.

The dining car was filled, and halfway through dinner the maître d'hôtel asked if we minded sharing our table. Not waiting for an answer, he seated a gentleman next to Father. The man looked to be in his fifties. He was large and pudgy, with white curls that twisted about his plump face like whipped cream decorating a pudding. A pince-nez, dangling from a cord affixed to his shirt, had left a red mark on the bridge of his nose. I noticed an odd gold ring on one finger and remembered my father once saying a gentleman should wear no jewelry.

"I apologize for intruding," the man said. "I know it can

be a great nuisance to have a stranger watch you consume every bite of food and listen to every word you say. It either paralyzes one or makes one say something *insensé*."

From my small store of French I remembered that *insensé* means "senseless."

"I'm Paul Louvois, but you need pay me no attention." His English had a strong French inflection, and he had dropped the French word into his English sentence like a man selecting a delectable bonbon from a box of stale English toffees.

Father gave Monsieur Louvois a tight smile and, after introducing us in the briefest of ways, went back to eating his fish.

Louvois appeared challenged by Father's reserve. Rather like an impudent child who longs for attention, he said, "That salmon looks *très savoureux*. I mean to eat well, for there will be nothing like this offered in the middle of the Syrian desert, where I am headed."

I could not suppress my excitement. "The Syrian desert! We're going there too."

Father looked at me. Only someone as attuned to his displeasure as I was would have noticed his irritation. I fell into an embarrassed silence.

It was too late. Monsieur Louvois's interest in us had

been piqued. He had seen Father's reluctance to discuss our destination. Mischievously, he asked, "Whatever will you do there?" His voice but not his eyes were innocent.

Father said rather dryly, "Surely you can't be surprised that, should a trip through the Syrian desert recommend itself to you, it might also appear attractive to someone else?"

If Monsieur Louvois was aware that his question had not been answered, he gave no indication and appeared, instead, forthcoming. "I do not like the desert," he said. "It is hot and uncomfortable, but to find what I am looking for, that is where I must go. I deal in antiquities."

"You say you 'deal.' For whom do you buy?" It was uncharacteristic of Father to ask so direct a question. He must have been uncertain of Monsieur Louvois, even suspicious— it was not only that the man was French, but he was also talkative. Father did not approve of talkative people. I had often heard him say, "The more words, the fewer thoughts."

"I have clients all over the world." Monsieur Louvois waved an expansive hand. "Galleries, museums, private collectors. People long to go backward in their imagination as well as forward. We don't wish simply to exist forever in some future; we wish to have existed in some distant past. It is satisfying to have a small memento of that past, and so they buy from me. I want to get to Palmyra and Antioch—

all ruins now, *déplorable*, of course, but they're digging up some things of interest."

Only a quick glance from my father kept me from saying that Monsieur Louvois had named the very places we were visiting. The Frenchman continued to talk about what he hoped to find. "One has to move quickly these days; the archaeologists are as common as sand flies."

Father said, "I rather thought it was a good idea to leave discovery to the archaeologists. I believe there is a preferred way to go about excavating these things so that they are not damaged. At any rate, I understand the Turks don't allow antiquities to be taken out of their country."

I wondered at Father's criticism and why he had taken such a dislike to Monsieur Louvois.

"I look upon the Ottoman Empire as a usurper," the Frenchman said. "I suppose you British would not agree, but we French think of many of the countries under the Ottoman Empire as a part of France's little family. With that point of view, what one finds belongs not to the Turks but to my country. The only problem, and it is not a small one, is that the Turks keep the traveler under their thumb. I have been told I cannot travel on my own. They want foreigners to follow about after one of their guides like a mother duck with a row of ducklings."

The waiter appeared, and I chose chocolate cake for dessert while Father stopped at coffee. Monsieur Louvois ordered his salmon. I waited for my father to tell him that he had met with the same rule against traveling in Syria without a Turkish guide and that we had joined a tour going to the very places Monsieur Louvois had mentioned. Instead, Father turned quite decidedly back to his dinner, forcing an end to the conversation; and before I had finished my cake, Father was excusing us.

"Why didn't you tell Monsieur Louvois about our tour?" I asked as we walked back to our compartments. The cake had been very good, and I was sorry to leave it.

"That man doesn't need to be encouraged. He acts as though we were both sitting in his lap. With someone like that one needs to create a little breathing space." Father appeared more than irritated. He seemed worried, and I wondered what there could possibly be about the amusing Frenchman that might trouble my father.

I awakened the next morning with delight, possessive of my little train compartment, which was all mine in a way no other room I could recall was. From its shelter I looked out my window and watched the snow-covered peaks of the Alps shift from blue to pink to gold with the rising sun. The train began its steep descent through a tunnel of green forests into Italy. I was distressed that all these wonders were sliding by so quickly. For a moment I thought of reaching for pencil and paper, but the idea of capturing in some clumsy sketch what I was seeing was as foolish as the thought of getting a lion by the tail. Besides, I was hungry.

When I stopped for my father on my way to breakfast, I found him in pajamas and robe. An empty cup and a plate of crusts stood on his nightstand. He explained, "I have some papers to read, so I've had my tea and toast brought to the compartment. You don't mind breakfasting alone." It was not a question.

I went on to the dining car both nervous and pleased at my independence. "What is that lake?" I asked my waiter. He was young with pale skin and feathery blond hair.

"We are passing through Stresa, mademoiselle," he answered, very conscious of maintaining his dignity. "That is the Lago Maggiore."

In a strange coincidence Monsieur Louvois entered the dining car moments after I did. He hovered beside my table. "*Bonjour.* May I join you?"

I would have preferred eating alone, for I did not want to miss a moment of the pictures that were speeding by the window. Unfortunately, I was not practiced enough to make a graceful escape. "Yes, of course," I said, but I could put no warmth in my voice.

"Surely you aren't going to be as *réservé* as your father. Perhaps you will tell me where you are going."

I saw no reason to evade the simple truth; besides, I found a wicked pleasure in talking with this man when I was sure Father would not have approved. "My father has some business in Syria."

So charming was Monsieur Louvois, and so flattered was I by his interest in me, that by the time breakfast was over, I had told him where I lived in London, how my mother had died, that my father was a solicitor (at least in that I was prudent), our entire itinerary, and the name of our travel agent.

"A solicitor in the middle of the Syrian desert," Louvois said. "That is most interesting. Perhaps I should contact the representative of Watson and Sons in Beirut and see about joining your *excursion*; it appears to suit my needs exactly. Of course, your father will not be happy to see me. He has put me down as a bore. But tell me, what is *your* interest in the desert? Perhaps you have some obsession I haven't guessed: a *penchant* for studying rare eagles or a desire to brush up on an obscure Arabic dialect?" He gave me a coy look across our now-empty plates.

"I sketch a little," I said, at once on the defensive.

"I must warn you that in art, my standards are *sévère*. I

don't like clever amateurs. I prefer people with no ability at all to amateurs who require you to spend time deciding whether there is anything in their work to which you must pay attention."

I was hurt. "You needn't give my work a thought. It requires no notice."

"The other thing with amateurs is their braggart's modesty." He laughed, and seeing that he was teasing me, I joined in the laughter.

Anxious for something to focus on besides myself, I said, "Tell me about your gold ring."

"It is an Egyptian scarab seal inscribed with the name of Thutmose III. The scarab is the dung beetle, you know. It lays its egg in a ball of dung, which it pulls up hills so that the ball may tumble down to find a resting place. The Egyptians linked the scarab to the sun god and the ball of dung to the sun's orb. I have always had a great *rapport* with a people who can couple something so earthy with something so heavenly. Now I must send you back to your father to plead my cause, for I won't have him deny me something as pleasurable as your company."

Guiltily I made my way back to my compartment, sure that Monsieur Louvois had been quizzing me for some purpose of his own and that foolishly I had given too much away.

IV

ISTANBUL

*a*T THE VENICE STATION I pressed my nose against the train window, but I was disappointed to find I could see nothing of the fabled city built upon the water. As we passed into Serbia, it was growing dark.

At dinner Monsieur Louvois was sitting at the opposite end of the dining car. Apart from a pleasant nod to us, he made no effort to renew our acquaintance.

"Thank the Lord for small favors," Father said.

I thought with a pang of guilt that if Paul Louvois had reason to be curious about us, I had already given him all he information he needed.

Father was in a talkative mood and chatted on about a trip he had taken to Arabia years before. It was a lively story involving camels and disguises, and I found myself laughing out loud at Father's descriptions. I could not remember another time when my father had made so great an attempt to entertain me. His efforts made me feel quite grown-up.

Over coffee Father spoiled it all by asking, "Well, Julia, what do you hope to get out of this trip?" Immediately I was transported to those terrible hours when my nanny brought me down to have tea with my father. Father would quiz me. "What did you and Nanny do today, Julia?"

"We went to the zoo in Regent's Park."

"And what did you see?"

"We saw a tiger."

"Do tigers have stripes or spots?"

A moment before, the tiger was vivid and alive in my mind; now I was uncertain. There followed questions about where tigers came from and what they ate, and little by little my tiger dwindled and faded and finally died altogether. Each time I went down for tea, I promised myself that I would not reveal what I had seen, so I might keep it for myself, but each afternoon I would be intimidated by my father into blurting out answers to his questions, so now when my father asked me what I hoped to get from the trip, I found myself answering the first thing that came into my mind. "I hoped it would be a chance to get to know you better, Father." The answer surprised me as much as it appeared to alarm him.

"Really, Julia, one would think after sixteen years you would know me quite well enough." Mercifully there were no more questions. At least, I thought, he remembers how old I am.

At last we reached Istanbul, where we would board the steamer that would take us to our destination of Syria. I had moved so far and so fast, I felt I had glimpsed everything and seen nothing. Now as I stepped from the train, I was aware of stepping into a world that had been made for others and not for me. Everything seemed strange. There was a spicy, ripe smell, as if the country were very ancient, as indeed it was. Men moved about in long gowns or pleated trousers. They wore turbans or fezzes. The sun beat down on me, warming my body; even the cobblestones I stood on radiated heat.

Knowing that Turkish customs officers would board the train, my father had taken measures to conceal any books or papers. Even our Baedeker guidebook was forbidden in Turkey.

"Why are the Turks so suspicious?" I asked.

"They are worried about foreigners bringing in propaganda to incite revolution among their subjects. Since there are revolutionaries like the Young Turks making trouble, I'm not sure they aren't right to take precautions."

I quickly looked around to see if any of Father's Young Turks were about with their troublemaking, but if a revolutionary was nearby, I could not discover him.

The officers inspected our passports and asked the amount of currency we were bringing in: *"Combien d'effectif?"* Father's reply satisfied them, and in a moment the officers had passed on to the next compartment.

My frustration at hurtling through countries and seeing so little must have been obvious to my father, for he apologized. "Just now I'm due in Beirut, but when we return, I promise to allow you a few days here in Istanbul." As a further consolation to me, on the carriage trip that took us from the train to the steamer, Father gave the driver a generous sum to pass the famous mosque known as Hagia Sophia.

I saw with awe how man had made the dome to stretch over his place of worship, as God had stretched the sky over man. In my amazement the only words I could manage were a weak "It's very large."

"For so meager a comment, Julia, I might have spared us the trip through these filthy streets."

I sighed, wondering if I would ever meet my father's expectations.

I had no sooner become used to the train than it was time to board the steamer that would take us to Syria. Syria was still nothing more than a name, for I had no pictures in my mind to go with it. I thought it a kind of miracle that in a matter of days I could go from one continent to another, and I wondered if my impressions would ever catch up to me.

When we arrived at the dock, Father spoke rapidly to the *douanier*, the customs officer, in a language I did not understand, handing him some gold coins. A moment before, the man had been ready to delve into our luggage, but this apparently changed his mind. The detour past the mosque had cost us time, and we boarded the steamer just as it was about to sail. There was some confusion about our accommodations, and Father, whose years in the foreign service must have prepared him for misunderstandings, shrugged good-naturedly and went to speak with the purser. I stood alone at the rail, staring greedily at Istanbul's seven hills, with their white domes and clusters of minarets aimed toward the blue sky like rockets. Seeing what I had not really seen at all, I felt like a child who has been given a shiny new toy only to have it snatched away.

"You look as though you are sorry to leave." The comment came from a young man standing next to me. He was about my cousin Teddy's age, tall, with ginger hair and hooded eyes that were amazingly blue. He seemed to approach me for the purpose of amusing himself, as if my response would not matter to him one way or the other. His look of detachment couldn't quite disguise an underlying impatience, as though he were putting off some extraordinary reward.

"I don't mean to trespass," he said, "but you do look terribly wistful. My name is Graham Geddes."

"I'm Julia Hamilton." I couldn't supress a sigh. "In the last few days I've traveled so far and seen so little."

"My experience has been rather the opposite," he said, and then he quickly changed the subject, as if he wanted to distract me from his first comment. "Surely you saw Saint Sophia?"

"But it's not a cathedral anymore. It's a mosque—Hagia Sophia."

"They've added on minarets and plastered over the Byzantine mosaics, if that's what you mean. What else did you see? The Hippodrome?"

"I'm afraid I don't even know what that is."

"It started out as a racecourse for chariots. Emperors were crowned there and the odd martyr burned at the stake." He saw my look of dismay. "Not your cup of tea? But of course—you are traveling to see only what will give pleasure."

"I am traveling to see everything that is worth seeing, whether it gives me pleasure or not."

"Touché," he said. "You mustn't mind my boorishness. I haven't had much practice in the social amenities these last weeks. Please don't go away. Let me practice on you."

"You needn't apologize," I said. "I freely admit to being uninformed and leading a sheltered life."

"I've heard my sister say the same thing, but I tell her people build their own shelters. She says I'm a pretentious snob, and so I am. Still, I find it hard to look at Istanbul and not remember that only a dozen years ago England and Russia turned their backs while the sultan ordered thousands of Armenians to be slaughtered here."

I shuddered. "You seem to know a lot about the past, and not very nice things at that."

"I'm studying history at Oxford, and history is full of unpleasant things."

"Those warships in the harbor don't look very pleasant," I said.

"Those are the sultan's. He sits in his palace looking out over the Bosporus, hatching his plots and trusting no one, not even his own navy. He doesn't allow ammunition on those warships, lest his own men turn the guns on him."

"Might they do that?"

"I fervently hope so." The anger in his voice surprised me. It was so strong, it appeared almost personal.

I didn't want to hear any more about warships and burning martyrs and slaughtered Armenians. Graham Geddes seemed to imply there was something to be done about such things, but if there was, surely we would not be the ones to do it. I was attracted to the young man in a way I couldn't explain. When my father talked about world events, it was so impersonal, I could never find my way into the events and quickly lost interest. Graham Geddes's emotion made me feel history was alive.

There was something else as well. I supposed it was my hopeless romanticism, but there seemed to be between us some other communication than the one we were speaking aloud, so that even if our conversation should stop, that secret communication would go on.

I became aware that the top button of my blouse had become undone, and I could not think which was worse, leaving it that way or awkwardly fumbling with it. I raised my hand to make some effort.

Graham Geddes had been watching me, and now he leaned over and fastened the closing. It was an impertinent act, but it was done so simply, he might have been dressing a child. He grinned. "Mustn't be untidy, must we?"

To cover my embarrassment, I asked, "Where are you traveling to?"

"I'm going to see something of Syria for research I'm doing at Oxford, although just lately I've been frittering away a few weeks in Athens."

I wasn't sure I believed him, for his answer sounded practiced, as if he had rehearsed it. There was some delay over the raising of the gangplank, to allow a pair of Turkish soldiers in smart uniforms and fezzes to come aboard. Graham Geddes's face turned ashen. He looked as if he might have to undergo a trial and did not have the strength for it. The soldiers were approaching passengers, most of whom looked like Turkish nationals, and asking to examine their papers. I was startled to see one of them approach Geddes. He recovered his composure and offered his British passport with as much nonchalance as a vicar's wife handing out a cup of tea.

The soldier painstakingly turned the pages, studying each stamp until one of them caught his attention. "You have come from Salonika?" I was surprised. Geddes had said he had come from Athens, not northern Greece.

"I am a student of history with an interest in the ruins of Macedonia."

The soldier appeared skeptical. "And now?"

"More ruins—Palmyra."

For a moment the soldier appeared to consider whether the answer was insolent, even suspicious. And then an odd thing happened. The soldier handed back the passport. "I have a cousin in Salonika," he said, and smiling at Geddes in a way that could only be described as sharing a secret, he added, "Salonika is a fine city." He saluted and turned on his heel. In another moment he had joined the other soldier, and the two of them were making their way down the gangplank. The steamer began to shake and lurch, and the strip of sea between the pier and the boat grew wider. I started to tell my companion that my father and I were going to Palmyra as well, but before I could get the words out, he excused himself.

I was alarmed at my reaction to this stranger. I had never felt so attracted to anyone. I wanted to go after him. He seemed to offer more adventure than the trip itself. The exciting thing was that he was my adventure and not my father's.

When Father joined me on deck, I asked, "Tell me something about the city of Salonika."

"Salonika is a nest of conspiracy. The Turkish sultan would like to get his hands on Süleyman Nazif and his revolutionary Young Turks, who are making trouble for him there. The Young Turks want to get rid of the sultan and take over the government of the Ottoman Empire."

"But I saw a Turkish soldier examine the passport of someone next to me, and he seemed more friendly after he saw the man had come from Salonika."

"That's a different story. Many of the Turkish solders are sympathetic to the Young Turks."

"Why is that?"

"I suppose they are tired of poor food and not getting paid. When the term of their forced service in the Turkish army is over, the sultan shoves them back into the army for another stretch. Why are you asking these questions? You're in a bit over your head, aren't you? By the way, who was the man you saw having his passport checked?"

"I don't know. Just some man." I did not want to share Graham Geddes with my father.

"Surely, pretending as you do to an artist's eye, you can describe him a little more fully than that."

"He was an old man with dark skin and white hair." It was the first lie since I was a child that I had told my father. It didn't make me feel guilty. I thought it a harmless secret and only fair that I should have a secret of my own: My father had so many.

V

BEIRUT

FATHER LEFT ME at our hotel, promising to be back sometime in the afternoon. He didn't warn me to stay at the hotel, knowing that in so unfamiliar a city, it was what I was sure to do. Stepping into the unknown streets appeared as dangerous to me as stepping into the middle of a river whose depth I couldn't guess. "I might just as well be back home," I lamented, and wandered out into the hotel garden feeling the whole city was for sale and I had no money.

There was little in the garden to cheer me. The stone bench upon which I sat was chipped and cracked, with aggressive vines clawing at its feet. I was surrounded by exotic plants, but they were all shabby: tattered palms, lemon trees with shriveled fruits, and forlorn shrubs with garish blooms the colors and size of gaudy china plates. Rustles and shakings under the foliage suggested there were

41

sinister, impatient creatures waiting for me to abandon the garden and leave them to their evil play.

Although the sun had been at it only a few hours, the sky was bleached white and I had to shade my book with my hand to keep the print from dancing. Everything told me I was a great distance from home. I was wondering what to do about it when Graham Geddes appeared, searching the garden as if he were looking for me. Yet upon discovering me, he feigned surprise.

"We seem to be staying at the same hotel," he said, then looked about. "Why have you settled down in this ghastly jungle?" His approach was playful, very different from his more serious manner on the ship.

With Graham Geddes's appearance the day brightened, like polish rubbed onto a tarnished piece of silver. "My father has some business this morning and I don't have the courage to start out on my own, but it seems a waste to sit still when I'm only going to be in Beirut for a day."

"Let me offer my services as a guide. I've been here before, and I'd enjoy showing off my knowledge."

I couldn't disguise my pleasure. "That would be so kind of you, Mr. Geddes. You are sure you'll have time? How long will you be in Beirut?"

"Call me Graham, please, and like yourself, only one

day. I'm going on to Damascus tomorrow and then on a tour to Palmyra."

"I wonder if it's the same tour my father and I are going on." When we compared notes, I found with pleasure that it was. "It seems half the world is on its way to Palmyra," I said. "We met a Frenchman on the train who was going there. Why are you taking the tour?"

"I'm not enthusiastic about tours: two weeks of enforced company with dull companions—present company excepted, of course—and a stuffy tour leader who knows considerably less than I do. But the Turks have made it a rule that no Europeans can move about unless they are under the thumb of one of their guides, and this tour travels near several Druze villages I wish to visit. The Druze, a religious sect of Arab peoples, are my speciality—their lives and mine are entwined. Now, Miss Hamilton, you must tell me why you are here instead of buying chic dresses in Paris."

"You must call me Julia. I'm here with my father, who is a solicitor and has business in Beirut. When I heard he was going, I coaxed him into taking me. It was all spur-of-the-moment."

"A solicitor?" Graham looked surprised and amused, as if he had just heard a delicious secret. "I gather your father knows people in high places. As he was getting into his carriage this morning, I overheard him give the address of the pasha, the ruler here in Beirut; one can't go much higher than that. I can only feel sympathy for someone who must attempt business in a town where business was invented: It puts you at a disadvantage of several thousand years."

Then, as if on impulse, Graham said, "I have to confess, I recognized your father when I saw him board the ship with you. I'll forgive you your little deceit."

Startled, I was embarrassed at having been caught. I wondered what Father would think when he learned Graham had seen through his disguise. And how, I wondered, did Graham know he was my father?

Graham answered my question when he said, "I knew your father was with the Foreign Office because I heard him when he came to Oxford to give a talk to us students on the Ottoman Empire. I disagreed strongly with your father's criticism of the Young Turks. I believe the Young Turk movement will bring democracy to Turkey and freedom to all the countries that Turkey now rules over with such tyranny: Armenia and Greece and the Arab countries."

There was so much emotion in Graham's words, I had the wild thought that he might be a revolutionary himself.

His face took on an angry flush. "I suppose your father is busy with cunning schemes for getting his hands on one more bit of land for Britain and is eager to thwart any plans the Young Turks might have for bringing a constitutional government to the Ottoman Empire."

I was about to scold Graham for his unkind words about Father when he said, "Enough about politics. What shall we do today? If we're going to be together, we might as well make a start. Perhaps we'll find right off that we hate each other, in which event we won't have to waste time on meaningless courtesies during the tour."

I was irritated by Graham's remarks about Father, but I managed to say, "I understand there's a mosque." I knew very well there was one, for I had studied it in my guidebook.

"Mosques and churches and temples. One would think tourists were all mystics on an eternal religious pilgrimage. Come along, then." The masterful way he took my arm and hurried me off made me wonder if our accidental meeting in the garden might have been part of a plan. I dismissed the idea as ridiculous, excited to be setting off on an adventure with someone so attractive.

As we made our way down the Place des Canons, the street that divided the city of Beirut, Graham kept up a pleasant chatter—half humorous and half informative. The few women on the Place passed us like shadows, for they were all in black, as if the whole country were in mourning. I don't know why, but their sight took me back to Durham Place and all those years I was shut away from worlds like this one.

There were coffeehouses along the Place, each one with its group of men sitting outside at small tables. As we passed, the men stopped their lively talk to look at us. I suppose they considered me a bold and wanton woman, walking as I was, unveiled and openly with a man. Their stern faces made me feel I was being judged by some standard I could not understand. I tried to be discreet in my glances, but it was hard to take my eyes from their odd and unfamiliar dress.

Graham said teasingly, "You must not think these people are in costume." He proceeded to explain how much one could tell about a man from what he wore. He adopted the manner of a bachelor uncle giving his country niece a day in the city. He was jolly and patient, producing little treats of information for me like twists of toffee. It was only when he thought my attention was elsewhere that he stole a look at me with something more than amusement—as though I were a book that might contain some scrap of interest if one could just get to the right page.

When we came to the mosque, Graham said, "We'll enter here. You must put these covers over your shoes." He approached a Muslim man who seemed to be guarding the door and spoke to him in Arabic. At first the man, looking in my direction, shook his head, but after a bit he saluted Graham in the Muslim way, moving his hand from his chest to his forehead in a graceful arc. Graham returned the salute, looking only a little self-conscious.

"I feel like I am living five hundred years ago," I said.

"And further back than that. According to the Muslim faith it is not 1907, but the year 1325. The Muslims mark their year from the time the prophet Muhammad fled from Mecca to Medina, thirteen hundred and twenty-five years ago."

While I stole glances at Graham, thinking him exceedingly handsome, he continued his lecture as he led me into the mosque. "You must not expect too much of this mosque; it's far from the best of its kind. The Muslims who captured it had to be satisfied with making over the Church of St. John, built by crusaders."

I thought of Hagia Sophia in Istanbul. "The Muslims turn Christian churches into mosques?"

"In Spain the Christians turned the Muslim mosques into churches. It's a resourceful world."

There were arcades and colonnades and little chambers and walls decorated with rough paintings of twining foliage and flowers. Hidden beneath the arabesques I could almost see the Good Shepherd and the image of Christ on the cross. Everywhere I looked, there was a feeling of one faith forever trying to elbow out the other.

After a while Graham said, "It's stuffy in here. We've done what you wanted; now it's my turn. What is needed is fresh mountain air and a view. I know just the place."

As we were leaving, Muslims began to stream into the courtyard and cluster around the fountain. I looked questioningly at Graham, who drew me into the shadows. "They are making their ablutions," he whispered. In a moment the men had disappeared into the mosque. "Listen and you will hear the imam call out."

"Allah!" Through the open arch we watched the men in the mosque kneel and touch their foreheads to the ground. The imam called out again, and Graham translated for me. "'The creator of this world and the next, of the heavens and of the earth. He who leads the righteous in the true path and the wicked to destruction. Allah!'"

In their eyes I was the infidel, and I felt it. Graham whispered that the imams once had not only been priests but served as commanders in chief of the conquering Muslim armies. "A sobering combination."

He ushered me outside, and I was aware of his holding

on to my arm a bit longer than necessary. There was some arguing over the fare with the driver of a two-horse carriage, but very soon the driver shrugged and saluted, and we climbed into the *yayli*.

"These people are so poor," I said to Graham, "I think you should pay what they ask."

"If you did, you would insult them," he said. "This fellow takes as much pleasure in our bargaining as he does in the money he will earn from the trip. In a proper bargain, both people gain honor." I folded my hands in my lap and remained quiet in the face of this hard lesson.

There was a warm breeze coming from the sea, but inside the small *yayli* it was hot. The driver explained that the top must remain up because the roads were dry and dusty. Graham and I were so close to each other that I could feel the warmth of his body, and when our hands brushed, our damp skin clung together for a moment.

We passed a garrison, the second one I had noticed. I wanted so much to understand all that I was seeing that I could not keep from asking questions. "Why are there so many Turkish soldiers stationed here?"

"Turkish soldiers are everywhere," Graham said. "The sultan is afraid of rebellion. He keeps his soldiers not only in Beirut but throughout his empire—Albania,

Mesopotamia, Armenia, Macedonia, Palestine."

"Why is he afraid?" I had never had so interesting or attractive a teacher at Miss Mumford's school.

"The Ottoman Empire once had a constitutional government, but Abdülhamid II put an end to all of that. Now, after years of the sultan's tyranny, the people are impatient to rule their own lands—if the European powers will allow it."

"What do you mean?"

"Germany, England, France, and Russia all have a foot in the door of the Ottoman empire." Graham pointed to a large building with a sign in both English and Arabic. "There in the American college they are turning out Protestants. The Scottish have schools for Muslims and schools for Jews, as well. The Germans are in the game with a very nice hospital and orphanage for Muslims. On the other side of the city the Jesuits and the Sisters of St. Vincent de Paul are doing their good works for France, and there is a Jewish college. As I said, everyone has a foot in the door."

It sounded to me like children fighting over toys, and I thought of Father and his trips to get and trade countries. It made me wonder what he would make of my escape with Graham. I calmed myself by believing that he would surely approve of all I was learning.

The *yayli* made its way along a winding road bordered with pines and small whitewashed villages where chickens were taking dust baths in the road. Goats ran beside our carriage like coach dogs. Women paused from drawing water, and men from plowing, to watch us pass.

When we reached Mount Dimitri, Graham helped me out of the *yayli* and sent the driver away, telling him to return in an hour. On one side of us was a small cemetery, on the other a grove of pines, and in the distance a city of white building blocks perched one upon another. Beyond the city was the sea. I thought even the finest painter could not invent such a handsome picture.

"If you know your Old Testament," Graham said, "you will know the Syrian gods are gods of the hills." He smiled at me. "Are you satisfied with your escape?"

I couldn't hide my delight. "I can't remember being so happy."

"That is an exaggeration, surely," Graham said, but he looked pleased.

He lay down on the grass, tilting his hat over his forehead to shield his eyes from the sun, and I settled next to him. Though there was no living thing about but the occasional bird, I felt very daring lying there in the open beside him for all to see.

"Can there be any place as peaceful as this?" I asked.

"Peaceful?" Graham said. "You should know that half the people who live here in Beirut are the survivors of massacres, drought, persecutions, hunger, religious wars, and tyranny. And if that weren't enough, we British and the Europeans are making plans for Beirut's future that have nothing to do with Beirut's welfare."

I sat up, indignant. "You are doing exactly what you did in Istanbul." Impatiently I asked, "Why must you see only wickedness?"

"I have never believed that innocence is its own protection; in fact, it leads to terrible muddles." He relented. "But then, I'm a confirmed cynic."

"I don't believe you are a cynic at all. I think you are someone who wishes he could change things, or why would you keep bringing up all that misery? Why would you care so much?"

He gave me a searching look, as if he wondered whether he could trust me. He must have decided he could, for he said, "I will tell you a secret, but under no condition are you to tell your father. I have just come from Salonika. It is a lovely city, with its sweep of waterfront, ships coming and going, the frosted peak of Mount Olympus, the church bells.

I went there from Oxford to talk with the Young Turks. I don't mean to brag, but they were impressed with my knowledge of the Druzes. The Young Turks believe I can help their cause in Syria."

Graham was losing me. "What is their cause?"

"The Young Turks are convinced that France and England mean to get a piece of the Ottoman Empire. They are against the sultan, but they are also fiercely opposed to other countries taking Turkish land."

"But what could you do?"

"They want me to travel through Syria pleading the cause of the Young Turks to the Druzes. They want me to assure them that under the Young Turks, the Druzes will be given their freedom."

So Graham was a young revolutionary! I looked quickly about, as if the sultan might be hiding beind a tree, ready to jump out and arrest Graham—and me, for listening to such talk. Graham's face was flushed with enthusiasm. "For the first time in my life I am working for a cause in which I believe: not England's colonial rule but democracy for Turkey. The Druzes will once again be free to speak their language, and to practice their faith as they wish; and I will have had a part in it." In his excitement he grasped my hand. "Why shouldn't I make a little history as well as learn it?"

Graham sat up and gave me a searching look. "I have trusted you with my secret. You won't betray me to your father?"

I shook my head. "I promise I won't," I said. I was flattered that Graham had cared enough for me to tell me his secret; still, I couldn't help feeling guilty. Wasn't Graham working against my father? I had heard Father say England opposed the Young Turks.

Graham must have noticed my worried look. "That's enough about the world's troubles," he said. "We're on holiday and should be talking of pleasant things."

"No," I said. "I want to know what you know. Why don't you start by telling me about the Druzes. Are they Muslims?"

Graham took off his jacket and, rolling it up, lay down again with the jacket under his head. He was so close to me, I could feel the outline of his body against my own. I tried to keep my mind on his words. "They are an offshoot of the Muslim faith, but they are not Muslims; at least the orthodox Muslims will have nothing to do with them. They give Muhammad no more importance than Moses or Jesus. Yet they worship with the Muslims."

"How can they worship with the Muslims when they don't believe what the Muslims believe?"

"The religion of the Druzes permits them to conform outwardly to the religion of the people among whom they live. Certainly that is a civilized attitude. In fact they are encouraged not to reveal their faith. Unlike the Muslims, they have no polygamy and the women are allowed to worship with the men and can even participate in the councils of the elders. The Druzes are a very honest people and are forbidden to tell lies—except to non-Druzes." He recited all of this in a dry voice.

"Are they a peaceful people?" I asked.

Graham said, "The Druzes are an impartial rather than a peaceful people. They have slit the throats of Turkish Muslims with the same gusto as they have beheaded Christians."

I shuddered. "I can't imagine why you study such people."

"My dear Julia, if I were to limit my studies to the history of those people who have never practiced violence, I would have to scratch for a subject. But there are much nicer things to do on so beautiful a day than talk of man's inhumanity to man." He reached up and carefully pulled out the pins from my chignon, and catching his fingers in my hair, he leaned toward me.

We heard the *yayli*. Graham drew away and I hastily did

up my hair. Graham's voice was matter-of-fact. "The driver is right on time, which means he will expect baksheesh."

"Neharak sa id," the driver called.

"Neharak sa id umubarak," Graham responded.

"What does he say?" My voice was unsteady as I fumbled with my hair.

"It is the Muslim greeting to someone not of his faith: 'May thy day be happy.' I answered, 'May thy day be happy and blessed.' But that is enough instruction for today. Please remember I am on vacation from school."

I caught the driver's half-amused, half-censorious look and blushed. I could neither account for my behavior nor regret it. I did not know how I would find a word to say on the return ride to the hotel, but as the *yayli* jostled through the crowded Beirut streets, I had my first look at a camel not in the zoo at Regent's Park. I exclaimed with pleasure.

Graham laughed at me. "There is no need for camels in this city. I believe they hire that beast to walk back and forth to give a false impression. Beirut is not a city of the desert, as Damascus is. It's an enormous assortment of men wishing to do business—very shrewd and ruthless men, as your father is no doubt finding out."

At the hotel I thanked Graham with what I hoped was a nonchalant word or two. Though I was trembling inside, I was determined to appear a woman of the world.

"No, it's I who should be grateful," he said. "You've rescued me from my own tedious company." For a moment Graham's air of detachment slipped, and he took my hand and said, "I'll be very pleased if I find we'll be together on the tour." With a mischievous smile he added, "And of course I look forward to meeting your father."

When Father returned to the hotel, I gave him a report of my day, stumbling over Graham's name, sure that Father could read my mind and see that I had listened to Graham's revolutionary ideas.

On hearing Graham's name, my father was obviously irritated. "Do you know him?" I asked, trying to keep my voice impersonal.

"When I was up speaking at Oxford, I heard of his interest in the Druzes and worse, the Young Turks. He made quite a speech after my lecture, and suspecting there might be trouble in the future from that quarter, I inquired as to who he was. I suppose Geddes recalls my being there. The unfortunate thing is that he will now know who I am. I'll have to have a word with him before he spreads rumors among the others on the tour. Under the circumstances I wouldn't see too much of him if I were you."

"How did your day go?" I asked, anxious to change the

subject before my father said more, for I intended to see Graham as often as I could.

"My day went exactly as I anticipated," he said shortly, then excused himself to dress for dinner.

Once inside my room I stood for a long moment with my back against the door as though I were keeping someone from entering. I let my hair down, trying to imagine how it felt to Graham. Though I had been traveling for many days, I realized I had just begun my journey. I saw that it could be a dangerous one.

VI

ON THE ROAD TO DAMASCUS

Miss Julia Hamilton
Hotel d'Orient
Beirut, Syria
March 30, 1907

Mrs. Edgar Hamilton
77 South Audley Street
London, England

Dear Aunt Harriet,

How I wish I could share this amazing trip with you. You would love Beirut, for it is truly exotic. There are Muslims in white turbans and green turbans and Muslims in kaffiyehs, which are a sort of scarf tied about the head with a cord. The Turks wear a tarboosh, and the Jews broad-brimmed black hats. You have only to look at a man's head to know his faith.

*At least you do if you have an instructor such as I
have. His name is Graham Geddes, and he is a student at
Oxford. He is very kind (although he pretends to be cross
and cynical). I met him on board ship, and he is staying at
our hotel. I was lucky to have someone to take me about, as
Father is always attending to some matter of importance
which he tells me is no concern of mine. Still, I can't help
feeling curious.*

*The weather is perfect. There are palm trees here,
and the oleanders and the wild roses are in bloom. From
the hotel gardens I can see the mountains on one side
and the bay with its steamers and flotillas of sailing ships
on the other. From this distance it is difficult to imagine
the cold March winds blowing over England and rattling
the shutters at Durham Place. The Julia Hamilton who
lived there has disappeared, and I'm not sure you would
recognize your new niece.*

*On the way to our hotel I saw the ruler of Beirut, the
Khalil Pasha, in his elegant carriage drawn by four
Arabian horses. It was like seeing King Edward driving
out on his way to open Parliament. I am sure I will come
home a much more sophisticated person with many
adventures to tell you about, but right now I am gullible in
the extreme and, but for Mr. Geddes's warnings, would*

have given away half my money in tips called "baksheesh."
Tell Uncle Edgar I am just teasing.

Your loving niece,
Julia

At seven the next morning Father and I boarded the train for Damascus. Graham was in a compartment two or three up from ours. When he saw us passing, he came out, a grin on his face, to introduce himself to Father. I could see he relished catching Father out in his game of posing as a solicitor.

Father acknowledged the introduction in a stiff voice. "I understand you were very kind to my daughter yesterday." Turning to me, he said, "You had better go and stake out a couple of seats in our compartment. I'll be with you in a minute." I was used to being sent off because my father had more important things to do, but this time, because it took place in front of Graham, I resented the dismissal more than usual and was glad that I had a secret Father didn't know.

When Father joined me, he had nothing to say about Graham. Leaving me to look out the window, he took up a book. The train made its way through small Muslim villages, up into mountains, and down again onto plains with apricot and apple trees and gardens bordered by hedges. "We might be traveling in England," I said, glad for a safe topic.

"There is something else that links us to England." Father pointed to a Roman aqueduct. "England shares a mutual conqueror with the Syrians—the Romans."

I was sorry that Father had spoiled the peaceful countryside with his tales of war. In this he and Graham had much in common.

At noon we stopped at Rayak for the buffet. The luncheon, a tasteless affair of chicken wings laid out on a bed of gummy rice, left us hungry, so as we boarded the train, Father paused to bargain for a melon with a startlingly beautiful young boy whose high cheekbones and angelic smile made him look, in his rags and tatters, like a disguised prince wandering among his subjects.

When we reached our compartment, Father found the slender blade of his pocketknife would not penetrate the melon's tough rind. His disappointment was severe, for I knew he had meant to give me a treat.

While he was struggling with the melon, a woman peered into our compartment as though she were studying us to see if we would make suitable companions. We must have passed her test, for after a moment she entered, pushing a number of large, battered boxes and chests ahead of her, then dropping down onto one of the vacant seats. The woman was about

Father's age, quite short and square, not fat, but thick and dense like a timber, with a tanned, weathered look suggesting something belonging to nature. Even her clothes, which were heavy tweeds, seemed fashioned of twigs and weeds. Under a felt hat that was clamped down upon her head like a helmet, her hair was gray and cut as short as a man's. Her eyes were dark and lively.

"I just got on at Rayak," she said in a breathless voice. "Sorry to crowd you with all this gear, but it's rather important, and I can't trust it to the baggage car." Seeing Father attempting to pierce the melon with his knife, she said, "I have just the thing for you." She began to grope about in one of her bags, pushing aside large sprigs of foliage.

She drew forth a wicked-looking knife. Taking it out of its scabbard, she gave the melon a whack, cleaving it into two large hemispheres. "There we are. Eat away."

She wiped the blade on her skirt and was about to replace it when Father said, "We are greatly indebted to your prowess, and by all means make another cut so that you will have a piece for yourself. I'm Carlton Hamilton, by the way, and this is my daughter, Julia."

"Miss Phillips. Edith Phillips. Please forgive my appearance—I've just come from Baalbek. I'm engaged in collecting botanical specimens for England's Kew Gardens. Some would have said this was Professor Ladamacher's territory, but I can assure you that London was here before Berlin. England's William Lunt brought a hundred and fifty specimens out of Arabia, and I am very close to exceeding his record." In a sober voice that scarcely concealed immense satisfaction, she said, "Ladamacher is dead now. Killed in a rather violent way by the Metawileh tribesmen." She used her large blade as dexterously as a fruit knife to cut away another chunk of the melon. "Delicious," she said. "I'm not sorry I've run into you. What are you doing here?"

Father winced at her directness. "My daughter and I are on a little tour of Syria."

"Charles Watson and Sons?" she asked.

With a deep sigh he said, "Yes, Watson and Sons."

Miss Phillips took no notice of his dismay. "It would have to be. They don't run more than a handful of tours in a year's time through this country, and Watson has the trade. After I learned the happy news that Ladamacher was out of the way, I decided I would move in to fill the gap. He and I had different approaches. He stayed in hotels and in the mansions of Turkish pashas, while I tramped through the desert to find my prizes, living in tents or under the stars, brushing away spiders as large as my hand. I despised Ladamacher for plucking the choice species from a land he neither cared for nor understood. I'm not sorry that the last glimpse Ladamacher had of this world was of a country he did not appreciate."

She looked furtively about as if there might be spies in our compartment. "There are those who say plants were not his only interest—that he was doing a little spying for the Germans. A few months ago he was botanizing near the railroad the Germans are laying down. But that is another subject. I knew the moment I saw you that you were going to be on Watson's tour. Well, you'll have to put up with me."

"I am sure you and your weapon will add greatly to our trip," Father said.

"I know just how you mean that," Miss Phillips replied, "but you'll find I can be useful." She launched into a story of how she had saved the life of a traveler who had become involved in a tribe's blood feud. "It was near Jebel el 'Ala, where there is a wonderful, unique *Iris stylosa.*"

I listened entranced. I, who could not recall meeting a single really interesting person in all my years, was now making the aquaintance of someone fascinating nearly every day.

Miss Phillips's story was a long one and led to another, about a journey in the Hadhramaut, which I gathered was somewhere in Arabia, and several more stories until Miss

Phillips interrupted herself to point out the minarets in the distance. "Esh-Sham, the city of Damascus," she said. "It was the chief city of Islam until the House of Umayyah fell. It is said that when the prophet Muhammad looked upon the city, he refused to enter it, not wishing to anticipate paradise. I was only twenty-four when I saw it for the first time, and I've seen it many times since, but I never get over the thrill. What is so satisfying about the city is that it continues to maintain the old Arab traditions: It is a city of the desert. Ah, here we are in the Beramkeh Station."

I stepped out of the station and into paradise! At the station the *Watson & Sons* sign was held aloft by our Turkish tour director with a certain hesitation, like the standard of a warrior reluctant to enter into battle. He claimed his small party and called the roll: "Miss Phillips, Mr. Hamilton, Miss Hamilton . . . ," and with a racing heart I saw Graham join us as his name was called.

With a great deal of bowing and hand shaking our tour leader introduced himself as Hakki Mahir Bey. "But for easiness you must call me Hakki, for I am going to be your good friend." Although it was a warm day, he was muffled and armored in a dark suit and a stiff-collared shirt. At first glance the round glasses on a round face, the slicked-back hair under his fez, and the slight frame suggested a schoolboy on his first visit to town, but a second look told me he was well into his thirties.

"They have sent a boy to do a man's job," Father muttered under his breath.

"I have a carriage waiting to take our party to the Hotel Victoria," Hakki said. "The other member of our group arrived yesterday. I am so relieved to have you all together in my hand. Please know this is not your England, and a wrong turning in this country is not without danger. We must all stay together. The important thing is that I do not lose anyone in my care." For a moment a look of panic came over his face, as if such a mishap would have terrible consequences for him; and, thinking of the dangers of the Ottoman Empire, I wondered if Hakki was something more than a tour leader.

Hakki plunged at once into his responsibilities. He told us, "I am sure you are tired from your train ride and you will want to retire to your rooms and make yourselves tidy." His eyes rested on Miss Phillips. "I will not bother you with stories now," he said, "but tomorrow morning we will meet after breakfast at nine exactly and I will tell you everything. In the meantime please when eating fruit, confine yourself to fruit that will peel: I understand the English stomach. Tomorrow for breakfast you will like our fig jam. Know that even though pork is not eaten by some of us, you will be able to get your rashers of bacon at the hotel. Sometime you must explain that word *rasher* to me. Believe that I am ready to learn at all times."

Watching Hakki make arrangements for our luggage, Father said, "I hope the man knows what he's about." I could see Father longed to take over and was having the greatest difficulty in his unaccustomed role of dependent tourist.

"He seems good enough at details," Edith Phillips said, "which is exactly what I don't wish to be bothered with."

When I reached my room, I looked about, delighted with the arrangements. The bedcovers and draperies were of silk—worn and patched, but a lovely shade of green, like water colored by the reflection of trees. On the floor were Turkish rugs woven into patterns of small flowers and leaping stags. Against one wall was a bench covered with silken cushions, fringed and tasseled and only a little dusty. I went through open French doors onto a balcony, where I could see the street vendors—water carriers and hawkers of bread and sweetmeats—all crying out in Arabic. The city was nestled up against the mountains, and beyond the mountains stretched the desert. The very word *desert* was enchanting. I felt that at last I had left Durham Place behind, and my escape was complete. Everything around me was so bewitching that at first I didn't see Graham standing on the neighboring balcony watching me, the expression on his face both amused and tender. The railings were low, and he had no difficulty moving from his balcony to mine. He laughed when he saw the draperies and cushions in my room.

"It's like a harem."

I said, "It must have been frightful for those women, shut away from the world."

"You're being a little smug, aren't you?" Graham asked. "After all, your own world isn't so different."

I winced. Father had not even wanted me to attend a university and had dismissed my wish to sit for the exams at Cambridge. *What good would that kind of experience be? University education is wasted on women who aren't suited for that kind of thing.*

Graham saw my reaction. "You see, just as I said. Men like your father colonize their women just as eagerly as they colonize countries. They conquer them and keep them in their place with their kindly oversight. It's time you think for yourself." I could see he took pleasure in stirring up yet another small revolution to trouble Father—this time right under Father's nose—but when he looked at me, he saw I was smiling. "What is it?" he asked.

I said, "I don't think you want me to think for myself. I believe you only want me to stop listening to my father and start listening to you. I don't see the difference." I could hardly believe I had the courage to speak up to Graham.

For once he was silenced. Miffed, he said, "I have an appointment. You'll have to see the city on your own today without either your father's or my instruction. That should please you." Seeing the disappointed look on my face, he appeared to relent. "I hope you will give me the pleasure of being your guide again very soon. I haven't forgotten our last little journey." A warm wind had ruffled my hair, and he gently ran his hand over it to smooth it. With that he climbed back onto his own balcony and disappeared into his room.

I was left with the view of the city, which without Graham seemed a little less enchanting. I told myself there were many days of travel ahead, and Graham would be with me.

That evening, when Father and I arrived together at the entrance to the dining room, Father was startled to see Paul Louvois in a white linen suit that glistened across the room.

"What the blazes is that Frenchman doing here?" Father hissed to me. We made our way toward the table where Monsieur Louvois was sitting with Miss Phillips and Graham. I was sure Father would have liked to dine apart, but a table had been reserved for the tour group, and it would have been poor manners to ignore our fellow travelers. Seeing my father's irritation, I was glad I had not confessed to mentioning the tour to Monsieur Louvois on the train.

Monsieur Louvois made the gesture of kissing my hand and then hastened to pull out a chair for me. He said, "I was explaining to Mademoiselle Phillips that I was here in search of beauty. Now I need search no farther." Graham shot an amused look my way. Father grimaced.

Edith Phillips, who obviously thought Paul Louvois pompous, brought things down to earth. "Monsieur Louvois says he buys and sells art."

Monsieur Louvois appeared irritated at the image of himself buying and selling. He explained to Graham, "I make little discoveries for museums and galleries."

"Ah, here is our schoolmaster," Graham said, "come to be sure his charges are not up to some mischief."

Hakki stood over us, counting. "Our party is all present. I am pleased to see you are eating together. Remember tomorrow morning, nine o'clock exactly. It might be best if you all took to your beds early this evening."

After Hakki left us, we felt like newly introduced children admonished by our parents to "get along nicely."

Miss Phillips said, "Well, we must make the best of this. For myself, I can get on with anyone—not that I mean to imply any of you are going to be a problem, but we must allow for the fact that we each have our own ways. You all must call me Edith. We are going to be much together, and we might as well be as comfortable with one another as possible. I am here to hunt plants for the Royal Botanic Gardens at Kew."

Father was amused by Edith. "I'm sure you'll have us all plucking daisies for you. As to why we are here, I think I can speak for my daughter as well as myself. We are here for nothing more than a little diversion, a distraction from the tedious profession of a solicitor, for my part"—Father avoided Graham's eye—"and an escape from the schoolroom for my daughter."

I had been relieved to have my father answer for me until I heard him describe me in front of Graham as a schoolgirl. My anger grew so hot that I hardly heard Monsieur Louvois speak of his search for the art of ancient worlds. When it was Graham's turn, he said, "I am here to do some scholarly investigation on the rather obscure tribe called the Druze." This time it was Graham who would not look at Father. The room was full of secrets.

Monsieur Louvois scowled at the mention of the Druzes. "Please do not forget to ask the Maronite Christians—those still alive because they were rescued by the French—how they like the Druzes who hunted them down not that many years ago and butchered them by the thousands."

"The French may have protected the Maronites, but it was the French who incited the Druzes." Graham had picked up a fork and accompanied his words with sharp thrusts at the tablecloth.

Paul Louvois's mood changed almost at once. "For myself," he said, "I am happy to assign such morbid investigations to someone else. Life is too short for assigning blame."

"Quite right," Father agreed. "We must leave justice to those who govern."

"That would be the last place I would look for justice," Graham said.

Father threw down his napkin. "I sincerely hope that our tour will not disintegrate into a series of dreary confrontations on matters over which we have little agreement, no influence, and from what I've been hearing, not a great deal of knowledge."

"I second that," Edith said. "I suspect we are all weary from our journey, and we ought to follow Hakki's very good advice and take to our beds."

In bed that night I was relieved not to be involved in Father and Graham's squabbles and hoped that before the trip was over, I would not have to choose sides.

VII

DAMASCUS

THE NEXT MORNING, when I stopped at Father's room on the way to breakfast, he announced, "I have no intention of subjecting myself to a 'tour' of a city I know perfectly well. I mean to visit an old acquaintance of mine."

Left to myself, breathless with excitement at the prospect of seeing the fabled Damascus, I set off to join the others. In the hotel lobby Edith was explaining that she meant to go her own way, but Hakki's obvious disappointment made her relent.

Graham—after first making sure I would be on the tour—informed Hakki that he, too, would join us.

"It is urgent that we keep together," Hakki said, leading us into the hotel parlor. He pulled the chairs together, transforming the parlor into a little classroom.

Edith placed herself firmly in the middle of the circle

and folded her arms as if prepared to challenge anything Hakki said. Graham, with an amused expression that suggested an adult about to tolerate a child's clumsy recitation, settled down next to me, resting his arm casually over the edge of my chair. Monsieur Louvois chose a chair on the edge of the group. He was elegantly turned out in a tan linen suit, miraculously uncreased. A paisley silk cravat was knotted about his neck. His white curls were still damp and grooved from their morning combing. In his hands he clasped chamois gloves, a white Panama hat, and a walking stick with a silver handle in the shape of a dog's head.

"I am going to tell you all about this city you are now visiting." Hakki flashed us an eager smile. "Damascus!" he announced, as though we might have thought ourselves in Bombay or Rome. "It is said Damascus is the oldest city in which people have always been living. If you recall your Genesis, you will remember that Abraham, who is our Ibrahim, and his servants pursued their enemy into 'Hobah, which is on the left hand of Damascus.' In your New Testament your Paul 'preached boldly at Damascus,' and here in this city he was let down over the wall in a basket to make his escape. Already one of our own little group, Mr. Hamilton, has made his escape. Ha-ha."

I was sleepy and distracted by Graham, whose hand had

slipped from the back of the chair onto my shoulder. Hakki's droning voice came and went in my head. At first the words were pleasant: Damascus was an oasis to the desert people; a city of streams and canals; a vision of the heaven pictured in the Koran, Islam's holy text; the home of the great princes of Arabia. But soon the voice became the voice of doom—the devastation of the city by Tamerlane, the burning of the Christian quarter. At last, with relief, I heard Hakki deliver a more immediate warning about the drinking water, and then he was leading us into the streets.

I looked longingly at the lively bazaars, sorry to pass them by, for in the life that lay ahead of me there was unlikely to be another opportunity. Hakki hurried us along to the Umayyad Mosque, which turned out to be not unlike the mosque I had seen with Graham in Beirut, only much larger and more ornate than seemed necessary. Hakki carried a long black umbrella, which he used as a pointer to catch our attention or as a standard to muster us when we strayed. "What you are looking at," Hakki told us with obvious pride, "was once a heathen temple over which was constructed the Church of St. John the Baptist. Indeed, it is believed by some Christians that the head of St. John once rested here. A mosque was then built in the church. For many years both Christians and Muslims entered by the same door and worshiped together, but for the last thousand years it has been Muslims only." The latter fact was produced as a recent bulletin and in an apologetic tone.

While Hakki pointed his umbrella here and there and told the story of the Muslim conqueror Musa ibn Nuair's triumphal march into the mosque with his four hundred Visigoth princes, crowned and girdled in gold, Monsieur Louvois slipped away from time to time to examine the pattern of a mosaic or the color of a tile. He did not seem able to keep his hands away from any object that caught his interest.

While he worried Hakki by playing truant, Edith bullied Hakki with questions of a morbid nature. "What do you mean by 'John the Baptist's head'? Do you mean the skull, or was there some mummification? If not, how could they tell whose head it was?" Edith had all the scientist's tedious insistence on detail, so the striking effect fell apart into a muddle of dull pieces.

Our eyes on Hakki's furled umbrella, we were about to ascend the narrow stairway of a galleried minaret for a view of the city when Graham held me back. "Why don't we leave Hakki to the tender mercies of Edith and Louvois and see something of the city for ourselves? We'll learn much more in the bazaars than in the mosque."

I was delighted to have the chance to visit the bazaars, whose many booths suggested what I had never before had—unlimited choice. To see it with Graham was a double pleasure. He grabbed my hand, and we ran away like two children, reaching the street breathless and, after the dark mosque, blinded by the sun. We stood for a moment until the world around us emerged from its dazzle.

I said, "You don't seem fond of Paul Louvois."

"He has a very greedy eye. I wouldn't be surprised if he didn't mean to roll up the whole country and take it home to France."

We fell into a more leisurely pace and were soon surrounded by small, ragged children demanding baksheesh. "*Ma fish*, I have nothing," Graham told them.

"*Allah yatik*," they replied good-naturedly. Graham translated this for me: "May God give thee." Graham appeared to be looking for a certain café. When he finally chose one, I assumed the reason he had singled it out was its pleasant location. The outdoor café was set in the middle of a garden with pomegranate and fig trees, whose leaves spread a dappled shade over the tables and chairs. Just below, a small stream wound in and out of a ravine. It was a pretty stream until you looked more closely and noticed it served as a deposit for broken bottles and clumps of concrete. The café was frequented by Muslims who sat cross-legged, smoking water pipes and playing some game that looked to me very like backgammon. The men did not look up from their games or their pipes, but I was sure they missed nothing about us.

"What are the pipes they are smoking?" I asked.

"They are nargilehs, or hubble-bubbles."

The proprietor of the café was perched on a stool near the kitchen, examining us through half-closed eyes. He was wearing European clothes and was clearly a Turk. I would have liked to sketch the man's face. It was all sharp planes and dark shadows, the face of someone to whom surprise would be impossible. As a waiter started for our table, the proprietor stopped him and, climbing down from the stool, came himself. Graham ordered two coffees and then said a few words I did not understand, after which the man did not so much leave our table as withdraw from it.

"What language were you speaking to him?"

"Turkish. I picked up a few words. I've asked him to join us. You don't mind?"

Of course I didn't mind. I could hardly believe that I was in this distant city, sitting in an exotic café with someone as charming as Graham, and about to share the table with a mysterious man.

The man returned carrying a tray on which were arranged three tiny cups of dense black coffee and a plate of six pastries. He produced a smile, but I didn't believe in it.

"Cream tarts," he said. "They are a speciality here in Damascus." His English was as thick and sticky as the tarts themselves. He pulled out a chair and sat down, offering the tarts with so much reluctance, I guessed that before bringing them out to us, he had agonized over whether one apiece might not do.

The man tilted his head in my direction as if to ask, Can we ignore her? Something in Graham's demeanor must have suggested they could. In English the man said to Graham, his lips hardly moving, "You are welcome in Syria. We have made contacts, and there will be help along the way." His voice hardened. "You understand we would prefer to do these things ourselves, but we are all known and watched by the sultan's spies." In a quick movement the proprietor finished his coffee, and with a curt nod in my direction he left the table, taking away with barely concealed greed the three remaining cream tarts.

When the man was out of hearing, Graham took my hand. I saw the men with the pipes cringe at the liberty.

"Was I right to trust you?" Graham asked. "I must have your word that you won't mention this meeting to your father."

"Of course you have my word." I was delighted at his sharing his secrets with me and happy that at last I was beginning to have a life apart from Father.

Graham stood up. "Now it's time I made good my promise to show you the bazaars." When we left, the proprietor was gone from his perch.

We entered the souk between enormous Corinthian columns. "Hadrian's Temple of Jupiter," Graham said. "Many civilizations were here before this one." The stalls that lined the maze of crooked streets sold flatbread; plump, sticky dates buzzing with flies; chests inlaid with mother-of-pearl; swords worked in silver; bloodred Turkish rugs; trays of rosy copper and bright brass scrolled all over with intricate engraving; piles of cucumbers and beetroots, walnuts and pistachios, fragrant cinnamon and cardamom; strange beetles and coiled snakes.

After I haggled over a length of pale green silk for Aunt Harriet and Turkish slippers with turned-up toes for Teddy, we came upon Monsieur Louvois, linen suit rumpled, chamois gloves shoved into a coat pocket. He was carrying on a conversation in rapid French with the owner of a stall where clay and bronze cylinders, no more than an inch or two in length, were set out on a frayed red velvet tray. When he spotted us, he abruptly ended his conversation.

"Ah, there you are," he said, a guilty expression on his face. "Hakki was *très douloureux* at your departure. Never mind. I too escaped, leaving the poor man with Edith, who was worrying him about the identity of a flower carved in the architrave above a gate. I felt sorry for the man; certainly she was punishing him, but for what I don't know."

"I don't think Edith cares much for Turks," Graham said. "I suspect that riding about the desert with Arabs has made her adopt the Arabs' anger at being ruled by the Ottoman Turks." Graham was anxious to get away, but Paul Louvois caught my arm and drew me into the stall.

"You must see these seals," he said, urging me. "Contracts here are not signed: A man puts his seal to them. This man has some very old seals that are *parfait*. Let me have the pleasure of buying you one." Hearing Monsieur Louvois's offer, the shopkeeper's fingers moved quietly as if he were counting.

"I thought you couldn't take old things out of the country," I said. I was holding a seal on which a leaping stag was carved. It was delicately done and I coveted it, but I meant to be honest and handed it back to the disappointed merchant.

Monsieur Louvois protested. "Something so small as that would never be noticed. It is only a trifle." When

Graham started to lead me away, he said in a rather nasty voice, "It is said that the British are honest in small things, but they do not hesitate to steal an entire country."

Graham warned him, "If you insist on carrying these things out of the country, Louvois, you will certainly end up in prison." When we were out of Monsieur Louvois's hearing, Graham said, "Cheeky, impertinent creature. He'll get us all in trouble with his cravings. The French think they own the Levant and can do as they please here."

As we passed the Banque Ottoman, Graham paused. "You don't mind if I run into the bank, do you? I'll only be a moment and you'll be quite safe."

More and more, I was seeing a secret side of Graham. I turned to explore a nearby stall where a young boy, who could not have been older than seven or eight, was sitting cross-legged on the dirt floor, embroidering a jacket. A man sat beside the boy, doing the same work. They had no light and their eyes were screwed up with the effort of working in the darkness. Impulsively I reached into my purse and took out some coins, which I handed to the surprised boy. "Buy yourself some candles," I said. The man snatched the money from the boy and secreted it somewhere among his robes. "My son does not understand English." He held out his hand. "Candles are costly."

I gave him more coins, but I knew the money would not go for candles.

The street boys had watched me handing over money and now began to worry me with pleas for baksheesh. I couldn't recall the words Graham had used to send them away and began to feel panic as they closed in around me, pulling at my dress and my purse. For the first time that day my eagerness to see the city turned to fear at how little I really knew about what I was seeing. I decided it would take many lifetimes to study so old a country, and then it would be just a beginning.

To escape the boys, I turned a corner. Immediately in front of me was a man in a tattered loincloth spinning in circles and howling at the top of his lungs. His body was filthy and crusted with scabs, his long hair was matted, and strings of spittle clung to his beard. His eyes were turned up so that only the whites showed. He threw himself down, writhing in the middle of the dusty road. He was uttering appalling guttural sounds, and his twitchings were bringing him closer and closer to me. I wanted to run, but a crowd was closing in around the man, blocking my escape. For one frightening moment all the distance between Durham Place and Damascus stretched out before me, an endless span with no return. I pushed rudely through the crowd and ran until I reached the bank, where I searched for Graham with no thought but my need to be with someone of my own kind.

Graham was at the counter, and I hurried to his side. He looked around, and for a moment, before he could mask it, there was an expression of irritation on his face. The man at the counter was leaning toward him speaking in a quick, low voice. "We will see that the funds are passed on to the Young Turks here in the city." He hastily returned Graham's passport, bowed slightly, and murmured, "*Es-salaam aleikum.*"

"*Aleikum es-salaam,*" Graham responded, and then he led me out of the bank. "You look like you've seen a ghost."

The man was still in the street, his cries and writhings more loathsome than ever. Graham reassured me: "Merely a dervish and quite harmless. They're a part of Sufism. An aspirant to the Sufi priesthood must serve in the lowest rank for one thousand days, and should he fail in the least thing in his training for the priesthood, he must begin all over again. Be thankful you belong to a faith that concentrates on forgiveness rather than perfection."

As I listened to Graham, I realized what it was that had nagged at me all day. It was the feeling that Graham's wish to be with me was not for the pleasure of my company but a desire to be seen with a suitable companion, someone who would allay suspicion. It was the same feeling my father had given me when he had said I might make the trip with him. I felt small and used, and all the pleasure and excitement of the day was gone. My disappointment was even greater when I reached the hotel and Graham hastily excused himself to hurry to his room. He obviously had no further need of me. I felt a terrible disappointment. I told myself that I should simply enjoy Graham's company without taking him seriously, but it was too late for that. I already took him seriously.

Abandoned, I wandered into the garden with some idea of wanting to cool off and came upon my father. He was sitting on a bench with a book. I said, "You look pleased with yourself."

"Why shouldn't I be? You are hot, dusty, and fatigued, while I am cool, clean, and rested. You can see which of us is the more knowledgable traveler."

"But I have seen something you haven't." I described the dervish.

"A sight worth seeing and no need to be frightened. They are merely one of the more showy forms of the Muslim faith. Sufism teaches that there are among the Muslims a very few who are in direct contact with God. Such men carry out the plan of God in the world by a kind of invisible government known only to themselves. There are times when I have thought Sufism a most comforting belief—the idea of the world in the hands of a secret few, busy doing what God wishes done on earth, with no need for us to involve ourselves. At other times it is a scheme that fills me with terror. But I don't mean to foist my little worries upon you. Instead, we should be looking forward to our adventure. Tomorrow night we will be sleeping in tents under the Syrian blue."

VIII

BY DRAGOMAN

A S WE SAT AT BREAKFAST in the hotel, an efficient Hakki handed around his agreement with the dragoman for everyone to see. A dragoman, Father explained, was a sort of native guide in charge of mukaris, who were the men who did the work. The very reading of the agreement seemed an adventure.

1. The dragoman, Abdullah el Feir, contracts to conduct Hakki Mahir Bey, agent for Charles Watson & Sons, and his tour group of five from Damascus to Palmyra via Jerud and Karyatein, returning through Forklus to Homs. The tour is to leave the morning of April 4.

2. There shall be provided four sleeping tents, a dining tent, and a cabinet tent. Six cots will be

furnished, plus tables and chairs, cooking and eating vessels, and clean mattresses and bedding.

3. Three mukaris, including one cook, shall be provided. The dragoman will hold himself responsible for the conduct and the honesty of the mukaris.

4. The tour leader will fix the hours of departure and halting.

5. The pay due the dragoman for each day of travel shall not exceed the amount agreed upon and will include the cost of the wages of the mukaris, food, horses, camel, donkeys, baksheesh, and all other expenses. One half of the amount due for the trip shall be paid at the beginning of the trip and the remainder at the trip's end.

6. In the event the dragoman is discourteous or does not adhere to this agreement, the tour director may dismiss him.

Abdullah el Feir   Hakki Mahir Bey

The talk of tents and camping out that had seemed so alluring in Durham Place now filled me with uncertainty. If it hadn't been for Graham and what my father would say about my romanticism colliding with reality, I would gladly have taken the first train for Beirut and home. I confessed to Edith, "I'm no good on horseback."

Edith, like me, wore a costume for desert travel: a khaki shirt and a divided skirt suitable for riding; however, Edith's jacket was composed almost entirely of pockets, all of them stuffed to overflowing with bits and pieces of plants. We both had heavy-soled boots. I had a straw hat with a wide brim, while the brim of Edith's crushed felt hat seemed to turn up and down at the same time.

"These hired Arabian horses will be very gentle," she said, looking expectantly toward the kitchen and brightening as boiled eggs and toast were placed before us.

I had other worries. "How do you manage washing up and all that sort of thing?" I hadn't been able to bring myself to ask Graham or my father.

"It will all be handled in the simplest way possible. Natural human functions are common to all of us, and high time you realized it." Edith, as handy with a knife as ever, deftly sliced off the top of her boiled egg and began to spoon out its soft center with a frightening ruthlessness. "You will discover there is nothing quite so fine as the desert and its people. They have a simplicity that is very attractive to me.

One can pack all one needs in a bedroll and travel for a thousand miles living on a bit of bread and a bowl of sour camel's milk."

"That's not a terribly attractive picture," I said, adding mischievously, "I can't think you would make do with a diet like that for long."

Edith, ignoring my remarks, spread a thick layer of fig preserves on her bread. "Enjoy your breakfast," she cautioned me. "You won't get another like it for a long time."

As I packed, I wandered in and out of Edith's room, inquiring as to what must remain in my trunk and what must accompany me, relieved to have her advice. Looking at the pile of luggage that was accumulating around Edith, I teased, "You're not exactly traveling with a simple bedroll."

Edith said, "All this is necessary: canvas bags for the seeds, drying paper, plant presses, bottles, boxes of shavings for any small shrubs I nip. Everything must get back to the Royal Botanic Gardens in the best possible condition." It was true that the bulk of her gear was for her collections. Edith's wardrobe consisted of little more than a flannel nightgown and a few pairs of pink knickers.

Edith said, "I pride myself on how little I require for myself, taking for my model the Bedouin. Their breeding of camels makes nomads out of the Bedouin. There is not much vegetation in the desert, so the Bedouin must move their camels from one small patch to the next." She sighed. "Reluctantly, I have to admit I am getting too old to wander about alone in the desert as I used to. I will never again have the feeling that I am seeing what no one has seen before me. Everything is becoming too easy, too accessible. One sad day the Arabs will awaken to find cities springing up in the desert and foreigners everywhere." Her voice took on a strange and angry tone as she said, "I promise you I will do everything in my power to delay that day."

Two carriages arrived to carry us to our departure point on the city's outskirts. Our trunks were left behind, to be sent on by railway to the city of Homs, where our first camping trip would end. I saw with disappointment that Hakki had arranged the seating in the carriages so that Monsieur Louvois, Edith, and I were in the first carriage and Father and Graham in the second. As everyone scrambled to be sure their belongings were put in the right carriages, Graham pulled me aside. "Remember, you have promised not to say anything of what you saw or heard yesterday. Perhaps I shouldn't have involved you, but I feel you are someone I can trust." He squeezed my hand and gave me a conspiratorial look. In my pleasure at his telling me he trusted me, I forgot all my suspicions of the day before.

I settled in next to Paul Louvois, while Edith sat opposite us with her various boxes piled up on the seat next to her, and prepared myself for what was becoming an endless series of amazing sights.

"What *rareté* do you have your eye on, dear Edith?" Monsieur Louvois asked. It amused him to treat the rumpled Edith with a show of deference due a duchess.

Edith brushed his mockery aside. "There is a quite lovely ranunculus that is said to grow in central Syria. I would love to get my hands on a specimen or two."

"For myself," Louvois said, "I never know what I am looking for. I like to be surprised. You of all people, Edith, know that if one looks only for the expected, one never comes upon the *singulier*." The banter was gone from his voice. It was one connoisseur speaking to another.

I shivered, sure that I would not want to get between either him or Edith and their discovery of the singular.

The carriages came to a halt in a ramshackle village on the outskirts of the city. A knot of Turkish soldiers lurked about on the edge of a cluster of huts. Beside the maze of huts were pens with horses, donkeys, and camels. When we rejoined the others, I asked my father, "We won't have to ride a camel, will we?"

"No, no. We'll be riding horses. We'll probably take a

camel along to carry our water and supplies. They're very useful—no hooves to be shod, only pads like a dog's. A nuisance in the rain, though; they can't manage when the land is slippery. Let's go over and meet the dragoman. I want to see how well Hakki has done for us." Father still did not trust Hakki.

The dragoman, a tall Arab whose narrow face was further elongated by a full beard, was regarding Hakki with a sardonic stare.

"This is Abdullah," Hakki said, introducing the dragoman. In his turn Abdullah summoned the three mukaris: Habib, Mohammed, and Mastur.

Mastur, the youngest of the three, had a pouting mouth and large, thickly lashed eyes. He was to be the *tabbâkh*, or cook.

Habib spoke with a whining voice suggesting that, even before the trip started, he was feeling put upon.

Mohammed was the largest of the men, a handsome, darkly tanned Arab with a closely trimmed beard; straight, aristocratic eyebrows; and deep-set eyes. There was a frown line etched between his eyes, as though he had been peering out over long distances in search of something that had never appeared. He was aloof and barely acknowledged our greeting, keeping his distance from the other mukaris as though he considered himself too good to be associated with them.

The dragoman, Abdullah, was very much in charge, striding about shouting, *"Yalla, yalla,"* meaning "Quick, quick," to the mukaris, who commenced loading the provisions.

Speaking rapid Arabic, Edith drew Mastur aside to show him how her cases were to be handled. She pointed to her specimen boxes and plant presses, but Mastur did not follow her gestures with his eyes, so I had the impression they were speaking of something other than Edith's gear. I wondered what these two strangers could have to say to each other.

I watched the supplies for our journey being loaded: heaps of tenting, piles of tent poles, cartons of food, baskets of linen, fodder for the animals, rifles, water canteens. The amount of luggage appeared to be an object of the mukaris' contempt. I remembered Edith's remark about traveling in the desert with nothing but a bedroll and felt guilty for bringing so much luggage. I had thought that after a day's dusty ride, I would want clean clothes to change into; and should there be no laundering in the desert, clothes would be needed for each day. I saw that my standards were too high, for even Monsieur Louvois had taken less than I had.

For the hundredth time Edith cursed the Turks' regulations that confined her to a tour group. "I would give a great deal to ride off on my own," she said, and seeing her determination, I wondered if I would ever have so much courage.

In an hour we were ready to leave. All my traveling across continents had led to this moment. I was leaving trains and hotels behind. My excitement turned into worry that edged into confusion. How would I manage? Graham must have noticed the look of panic on my face, for he strode over to help me onto my horse, boosting me onto the saddle with strong arms and leaving his arm around my waist for a long moment.

Habib climbed upon the crouched camel, pummeling it until first its back legs unfolded and then its front legs. It rose up to its full height and began to lurch forward in an uncertain preening gait like a child in its mother's high heels. The camel's saddle was tricked out in brightly colored tassels and bells. Edith had told me that the Arabs had four thousand words to describe a camel. The arrogant tilt of the camel's head suggested it took pride in that fact.

I watched the spectacle with delight, all my discomfort and apprehension forgotten. Abdullah on a great black stallion followed Habib, and after him rode a determined and uncomfortable Hakki, looking over his shoulder from time to time to count his little party. Father came next. I was prepared for the accomplished picture he presented, for I had a remote memory of seeing on my mother's dresser a photograph of my father on horseback with a pack of hounds. Watching his easy handling of the horse, I guessed with regret that there was much of my father's past that I knew nothing about.

Edith, competent and firmly in control of her horse, rode just behind Father. Monsieur Louvois was an awkward horseman but appeared so indifferent to his deficiencies that he could have been on a giraffe and it would not have mattered to him. He was followed by me, feeling very uncertain, and finally Graham, completely at ease on his mount. Trailing the party were the pack mules and the two remaining mukaris, who were seated on aged and skeletal horses. The mukaris regarded us with looks that implied it was hard to be under the yoke of fools.

The day began cool and pleasant. As we rode along, Graham brought his horse next to mine. "Why do these men stare so at us?" I asked him.

"They don't understand all these preparations for a few days' amusement, and they consider us spoiled children," he said. "Which we undoubtedly are."

I was encouraged by how compliant and responsive my little horse was. I had asked the mare's name and was told by

Mohammed: "Madam, our beasts are not named. It is enough that we have names."

"What is the Arabic word for silver?" I asked Graham.

"Fadda," he said.

"That suits her perfectly." She was gray with a shiny coat. "She's so docile."

"Oriental horses are very manageable," Graham told me. "They don't even require a bit. You'll find they go at a walk and not a trot."

Father had been watching us, and now he dropped behind to join us, questioning me as to how I was managing. After that, much to my regret, he took Graham's place at my side.

At first we rode among fields of wheat, and apple and peach orchards. I could smell the fragrance of the blossoms on the light breeze. Gradually the trees dwindled and the fields became less green. In the middle of the morning, after passing a small garrison of Turkish soldiers, we came to the village of Adra, where Mastur handed around figs, dates, slices of goat cheese, and cups of tea made with water that, to save our own supply, he got with baksheesh from the village well. I had eaten many large and elaborate meals, but none so delicious as this spare one.

In spite of the money that changed hands, the townsmen

gave the water grudgingly. I noticed how time and the rope had worn a groove in the side of the well.

Edith oversaw Mastur as he made our tea, even contributing some of her precious store of China tea. She announced cheerfully, "In the desert men kill over water. And quite rightly. It's what keeps them alive."

"The water or the killing?" Father said, receiving a cold stare from Edith.

Paul Louvois and Father strode off to talk with one of the villagers, while Edith wandered into the fields and Graham was deep in conversation with Mohammed. I was left with Hakki, who was clearly alarmed at watching the others stray.

"Hakki, why are there so many Turkish soldiers about?" We had met repeatedly with small contingents of soldiers who regarded us suspiciously.

"There are no more soldiers than are needed." Hakki answered me automatically, concentrating on Edith, who was now no more than a khaki speck in the distance. He could not contain his worry. "I am unhappy when one of you wanders away," he said petulantly. "I must know at all times where you are."

"But why are so *many* soldiers needed?" I persisted.

"We have always some well-meaning foreigners who

think they must sow seeds of discontent among the Arabs, telling them that this group or that will give them independence. We Turks understand these foreigners want our land for themselves, but the Arabs, being naïve, don't see behind such promises. Now, if you will excuse me, I will go in search of Miss Phillips."

Graham and Mohammed had been squatting on their heels, talking rapidly to each other. When Abudullah called Mohammed to some task, Graham joined me. I asked, "Does Mohammed speak English, or were you speaking Arabic to him?"

"Mohammed comes from a family that deals in hemp. They sell all over the world, so they know a number of languages."

"Why has he taken a job as a mukari?"

"There was some trouble—nothing serious, I'm sure. His family wanted him out of Damascus for a bit."

I thought there was more to it than that, but this time Graham would not confide in me.

Hakki rounded up Edith and called out, "Gentlemen and ladies, we have much ground to cover, so I respectfully request that you prepare yourself for the next stage. And please let us all be close to one another."

Leaving behind everything green, we headed toward

flat rocky country, riding along the dry course of what once had been a stream. "They are called wadis," Graham told me. I saw with a leap of my heart that at last we were truly in the desert. It was not the stretch of sand I expected, but a wilderness of stone.

Graham pointed. "Over there," he said. "You can just see them." Silhouetted against the dark blue of the sky was a camel caravan moving slowly toward us. As it drew closer, we could hear the bells and make out a dozen camels with their riders, all in black robes and headdresses. The members of the caravan passed us with no more than a curious glance. No words were exchanged between them and the mukaris. "Not of their tribe," Graham said. "In the desert, courtesy has very little to do with polite exchanges and everything to do with avoiding murder."

"How do they find their way? It all looks the same to me: just rocky piles."

"The Arabs have names for every inch of the desert. What is incomprehensible to us is plain to them. I wish I were here alone with Mohammed instead of tethered to this crew—your father watching me with a gimlet eye; Louvois up to Lord knows what mischief; Edith choosing one of the rockiest, most arid places on earth to pick her flowers. If it weren't for your company and those ever-present Turkish soldiers who would be after me in a flash, I would be tempted to take off."

I was pleased that Graham was happy to have me there, but I was not sure I liked being paired with the Turkish soldiers. We stopped for lunch among the remains of a village. "Mathna el-Maluli," Hakki announced, like a train conductor.

"Lately fallen to ruin," Abdullah added.

"Several hundred years ago," Hakki explained.

"That is as yesterday," Abdullah said.

"There will be lunch and we will all rest for a bit," Hakki ordered. "There is no point in traveling in the hottest part of the day." He acted as if he were firmly in control and giving orders to Abdullah, when the stop had been Abdullah's idea.

"The noon heat is bad for the horses," Abdullah had said. His concern was for the horses, not the riders. Habib hobbled the camel and sent it to graze on a handkerchief-size patch of green. After a while I could hear it belching as it brought up its cud, followed by the grinding of its great yellow teeth.

Mohammed gathered thorn branches and built a fire. Mastur set bread to baking in the ashes, and after roasting the coffee beans, he ground them in a mortar. The mukaris did not hurry, yet everything necessary was done. When lunch was ready, Graham, ignoring Father's displeased glance, sat next to me. "I must admit it gives me a certain perverse pleasure to irritate your father by paying attention to you."

I smiled. "It's not very complimentary to be told you are spending time with me just to anger my father."

"Believe me, if I didn't enjoy your company, even that pleasure, great as it is, would not tempt me."

I had to be satisfied with that small compliment. It began to worry me that Graham was becoming so important to me, for I felt sure I was not that important to him.

It was still blistering hot when we started up again—not the sultry heat you sometimes have in England but the dry, hot heat of a furnace. The trail narrowed, but our horses were sure-footed along the rocky path. From time to time we would meet a small band on camel or horseback. Sometimes the riders would pass with barely a glance, but sometimes they would stop and stare openly, calling out a few distant words that might have been either quarrelsome or welcoming. As the afternoon wore on, our little tour group fell silent with heat and fatigue. We rode along, our parade of shadows giving the journey a timelessness. I thought it might be the present or it might be a thousand years earlier, when desert travel was rare and fraught with danger.

IX

JERUD

ℭT LAST WE SAW THE outline of trees ahead of us. The horses began to quicken their gait. The trees became more trees, and there were gardens as well. Bit by bit the village of Jerud unfolded before our eyes like the paper flowers you drop into a glass of water.

As we approached Jerud, we saw a small lake, but the horses, wiser than we were, did not slow. Abdullah explained it was a salt pond. Minutes later we came to a stop just outside the gates of the village. Under Abdullah's direction canvas was stretched upon the ground, stakes hammered, and poles fitted. Within minutes Edith and I were in the tent we were to share, where I could see nothing more than two camp beds covered with a few quilts. "It seems sparse," I said.

"That is its virtue." Edith examined the spartan surroundings with relish. "You'll soon get used to camping and learn to like it. What people don't understand is that the greatest luxury is to do without. If there is anything I have learned from the Arabs, it is that most of the things with which we surround ourselves have more to do with the needs of other people than with our own."

The more I thought about Edith's words, the more sense they made. In Durham Place I had been all but buried in a large home overflowing with possessions. My life had been all routine and dullness. Here I was in a tent with nothing to call my own but a cot, and my world was full of adventure.

As we were talking, we could hear raised voices. Edith pulled back the flap of the tent and then reported, "Turkish soldiers in a shouting match with Hakki and our dragoman, Abdullah." Alarmed at the raised voices, I would have chosen to stay in the tent, but Edith went marching out, and I felt it would be cowardly not to follow her. Abdullah at his fiercest was shaking his fist at one of three soldiers, who was in turn gesturing with a rifle. Hakki, looking smaller and more ineffectual than ever, was hopping from foot to foot in frustration. After listening for a moment to the quarrel, Edith translated for me. "The soldiers are asking to see our papers, and Abdullah insists we are under his protection and should not be harassed. Hakki appears to be on the side of the soldiers and is trying to convince Abdullah that we should do as they say."

Father must have wanted to get the unpleasantness over with, for he approached one of the soldiers and handed over his papers. "I believe this is what you are asking to see." He said it with such commanding dignity that both Abdullah and the soldiers fell silent. The soldier examined Father's papers and then accepted Monsieur Louvois's and those of the rest of the tour in turn. When they had completed their check, they saluted Hakki and, giving Abdullah a menacing look, rode off.

Abdullah, with no regard as to whether the soldiers could hear him, spat and cursed. *"Kilâb."*

"'Dogs,'" Edith translated.

A pale Hakki walked over to Abdullah and quite bravely said, "You will have all of us in prison." Abdullah looked as though he might kill him, but Hakki must have realized that his future would depend on whether he allowed himself to be intimidated. "There is still work to be done," he told Abdullah. "A tent lacks a pole, and there are supplies to be unloaded." This call to work seemed to have some effect, and Abdullah strode away.

Edith took up her specimen box. "I'm going off to see what I can find in the fields. Here in the desert a plant goes through its cycle from flower to seed in a week's time and one has to move quickly." Mastur was hammering the last stakes for our tent. When he saw Edith leave with her equipment, he walked over to Hakki and began to argue with him on some point, finally leading him off in a direction that shut Edith off from Hakki's view so that Hakki could not see Edith leave the group. I was sure Mastur was distracting Hakki on purpose, but I merely supposed that Edith didn't want Hakki calling after her to return.

Our tent had been pitched so that its opening allowed the breezes to enter, but late in the day the direction of the wind changed, and under the afternoon sun I found the tent so stifling, I started out on a walk. The sun beat on my back and crept under my wide-brimmed hat. A hot wind nipped at my skirts. The heat and the miles of nothingness made me giddy. At first I could not understand Edith's optimism, for I saw only rocks, until I looked more closely and discovered small flowers nestled among the stones: miniature blue hyacinths and purple crocus and periwinkle—common flowers in England, but in a desert setting exotic. I had never been much attracted to nature, preferring to sketch man-made things like ruins of civilization. Now, caught up in Edith's enthusiasm, I examined a white cyclamen with swept-back petals. Among the barren rocks of the desert, its delicacy was reassuring. If such tender flowers could survive in such a setting, there was hope for me.

On impulse I took the cyclamen to the tent to sketch and found with relief that Habib had moved the tent to attract the afternoon breezes. Lost in my work, I scarcely noticed that an hour passed before a noise I hardly heard made me look up. I saw a small mouse and then another and another. They jumped rather than ran, as if they were propelled by springs. When one hopped onto my sketch pad, I ran for Mastur, who looked into the tent and laughed. *"Yerbu,"* he said, nodding his head, and he was about to leave as if all I wished were the name of the creatures.

"Chase them away," I ordered. "I won't be able sleep with mice bouncing all over me."

"They do no harm. The only bad thing is they bring the snake who wants them for his dinner." He departed, impatient with this frivolous demand on his time.

Thinking of the snakes, I heaped sand and rocks around the circumference of the tent to pin its hem to the ground, but Mastur's indifference was reassuring, and I began to be fond of the bouncing mice, losing myself in my sketching until it was time for dinner.

As I joined the others around the fire, Hakki said to me, "Why does Miss Phillips not come?"

When I said, "She went out several hours ago to look for

specimens," Hakki looked as though he might cry.

"I have begged all of you to stay together," he protested. "How could this happen?"

Monsieur Louvois said, none too kindly, "I would not have expected Edith to be late for a meal."

"Come and sit down, Hakki," Father said. "There isn't a desert that exists in which Miss Phillips could lose herself."

Still we kept our eyes on the horizon, waiting for Edith's substantial figure to appear, but there was nothing to be seen but the faint white houses of the village like empty squares cut into the purple sky.

Monsieur Louvois asked Hakki, "Why did that *petit fonctionnaire* insist on seeing our papers?"

Hakki said, "There have been rumors of people making trouble for the sultan in these parts. The soldiers must keep some sort of order to prevent a handful of troublemakers from sowing the seeds of revolution." He looked at Graham suspiciously.

The desert air had chilled, and seeing me shiver, Graham had edged close to me, taking off his jacket, still warm from his body, and wrapping it around my shoulders. He was so close to me that I could feel him shifting uncomfortably under Hakki's stare, but he answered in a strong voice. "I wouldn't call it revolution," he said. "I am sure there are those who simply want what many nations have and what Turkey once had—a democratic government."

"It's not that simple," Father said. "Suppose your seekers after democracy are successful in overthrowing the sultan. Do you think for a moment that the Arab world, when it tastes its first freedom in centuries, will be satisfied to remain a part of the Turkish government? No matter what concessions Turkey gives them, they will want their own country. The same is true for the Greeks and Armenians and Jews." Father's voice was intense and angry, as if he had been waiting for the moment when he could openly oppose Graham. "These people, and I suppose you are speaking of the Young Turks, will have opened a Pandora's box. It is not in oppression but in the first taste of freedom that revolutions arise. When the Arabs and the Greeks and the Armenians begin their fight for independence, your Young Turks will come down harder on them than the sultan ever thought of doing.

"Not only that. Once the Muslims come to power, they will impose their religion: Only Muslims will be allowed to hold office. Islam is the state and Islam is the religion. What will happen then to your Druzes, who have their own religion?"

I could not follow Father and Graham's arguments. It seemed to me that every solution would just cause another problem.

Like me, Hakki was not listening. He was looking out toward the desert for some sign of Edith, who seemed all but forgotten in the surly discussion. Now he said, "I must see to our dinner. Perhaps by then Miss Phillips will have returned."

Worried over Edith's absence and edgy from the men's quarrels, I hardly tasted the dinner of rice and mutton. Even before we finished, Hakki ordered Abdullah and the three mukaris out to look for Edith. When Father, Monsieur Louvois, and Graham insisted on going as well, Hakki became upset, pleading, "I have begged over and over that we stay together. I cannot have you going off into the desert for whatever reason." But they went.

Alone in my tent I was almost grateful for the company of the bouncing mice, who were now hopping about in my bags and shoes. Any moment I expected to see Edith march purposefully into the tent, complaining that too much fuss had been made over her. From time to time I stood at the entrance of the tent looking into the awful space of the desert for some sign of Edith, but the searchers returned without her. First Father, Monsieur Louvois, and Graham, and then Mohammed, Habib, and Mastur, and finally Abdullah. The whole party fell silent with concern.

"The will of God," Mohammed said, and Habib nodded. Only Mastur seemed unworried, and I recalled how he had distracted Hakki to keep him from noticing Edith's departure.

A frantic Hakki anounced, "In the morning we will round up the men in the village and pay them to search with us. I will wait up tonight."

I was grateful to Father when he said, "We will all wait up," for I was too worried about Edith to sleep.

The tents were hung with lanterns in the event that Edith tried to find her way back. No one left the fire, although from time to time one of the watchers dropped off for a few moments' sleep. I was wrapped in a blanket to keep out the chilly night wind that blew across the desert's cold stones. A terrible howling and whimpering cut through the darkness, and I shut my eyes, afraid of what I might see.

"Most likely a jackal," Graham said, secretly finding my hand in the folds of the blanket to comfort me.

When I opened my eyes again, I saw a star shoot across the sky, and in spite of my fear I called out in pleasure.

Father heard me and, using that as an excuse to move closer to me and Graham, said, "The Muslims believe there are satanic legions called 'jinn' that try to discover the secrets of heaven. To discourage them the good angels pelt the jinn with stars."

It was nearly midnight when two men on camels moved like specters into the light of the campfire. Without waiting for their camels to kneel, the men, each carrying a rifle, sprang down to the ground and saluted the party. They looked as if they were playing some part that was agreeable to them and that they had rehearsed. One of them kept in the background, but the spokesman's face was clearly visible by the light of the fire. It was a round, fleshy face, almost boyish in its smoothness, and beardless except for a wispy tuft of chin hair. The man's large round eyes had a surprised look. When he turned his head slightly, I noticed with a start a jagged scar like a slash that stretched across his throat. Abdullah greeted the men. *"Es-salaam aleikum,"* he said.

"Aleikum es-salaam," returned the spokesman, who said his name was Asad and that he was from the Metawileh tribe.

A cold shiver went through me as I remembered Edith telling us it was the Metawileh tribe that had killed her enemy, Professor Ladamacher.

Asad asked, "Your party is a small one. Is this all?" He spoke in heavily accented English. When he lapsed into Arabic, Graham translated for me.

Abdullah had been lounging by the fire, but now he sat up stiffly. "There is one other, a *hurmeh*."

"A woman," Graham translated.

"The *hurmeh* is not here?" the spokesman asked.

"As you see," Abdullah replied.

"Perhaps it is quieter thus," Asad said. "Not all *harîm* have the gift of silence."

"Unhappily, that is so," Abdullah said.

"It may be that we have found the *hurmeh*. It is possible we could bring her to you, but her discovery has been an inconvenience for us, tiring our camels and exhausting our water. For that you would doubtless wish to give us a little reward, although we could not accept it since you are friends."

Monsieur Louvois spoke up. "We will give you no money for the mademoiselle, but if you bring her to us *tout de suite*, I will give you something for the trinket you are wearing around your neck in exchange for the *hurmeh*'s return."

Asad replied, "Five of the gold coins of your country for our trouble. I could not sell the amulet, but it will be a gift for you in exchange for your generosity."

Monsieur Louvois handed the man the sovereigns and received from him a small ivory amulet that the man had worn on a cord. "If you have any other trinkets such as this one, you will find us in Karyatein in a day or two."

"We will find what will make you happy. Now we will return to you the missing member of your party."

After an hour of anxious waiting we heard Edith's angry voice complaining to Asad, who accompanied her, that she could have made her way back on her own. I was relieved to hear her voice, for I had had frightening images of Edith bound and gagged and slung upon a camel. Instead, when Edith appeared, she was riding the camel of the second man, who was not to be seen.

"My friend has been generous and given the *hurmeh* his own camel to ride," Asad said.

Edith, perched on the top of the beast, looked down at us. "Generous, my foot. He chose not to come. I told him he must ride pillion, as I would not; it's a most uncomfortable way of hanging on to a camel. I hope this thief has not talked you into giving him baksheesh for my return; if so, I have warned him I will report him to the next soldiers we see."

"We didn't give him a sou to return you," Louvois said. It was the literal truth, but it sounded unchivalrous.

The Metawileh couched Edith's camel and offered his hand, which she refused, getting down quite nimbly on her own. "I must in all truth say that you gave me a good dinner.

In return, you will be pleased to know, while you were gone and the man you left me with was asleep, I aired out the bedding in your tent, which was full of lice. I only hope I haven't brought them back with me. Some of your bedding was simply too disgraceful, and I tossed it into the fire."

Abdullah smiled. "We will give you back your amulet and you may have the *hurmeh*." But before he had finished his offer, the Metawileh hurriedly turned the camels toward the desert.

"Well, it's all my fault, of course," Edith said. "I'm afraid I've given you a great deal of trouble. I found a ranunculus quite unknown to me, and since one specimen is not proof enough, I went looking for another. In my excitement I must have become disoriented. Asad and his friend, Faiz, and another man, Yusuf, kindly—or so I thought—took me in and fed me. Just when I expected that they would bring me back here, Asad and Faiz disappeared, leaving me with Yusuf. Of course I was onto their game of ransom at once, but I was reluctant to start off in the dark, not knowing how far from camp I was."

Hakki was torn between relief at having Edith back and dismay over her disappearance. "Miss Phillips, I most humbly entreat you never, never to leave our group again. I have said over and over that we must stay together, and here on our first night in the desert you vanish from me."

Edith said, "I give you my word, Hakki, that hereafter I will stay near the camp." But no one, least of all Hakki, believed her.

I was puzzled. The men obviously had been asking for ransom in return for delivering Edith, yet all the while Edith appeared to be the one in control. I felt I had been present at the performance of a little play, but I could not figure out the characters or the plot. Still, I was so pleased to have Edith safely back in the tent with me, I put my suspicions aside. Even the mice scurrying about seemed less a problem with her there. "We were worried," I said.

Edith sat down on her cot heavily. "I was never in any danger, but it's been a long day." She appeared strangely exhilarated.

"More than a long day, surely," I said. "If I had been you, I would have been terrified."

"You are safer in the desert than on the streets of London."

"But you were lost. What if those men had not come along?"

"But they did, and I am grateful to them. They kindly took me in, and if they made a little money from their hospitality—for I don't believe for a moment that ransom wasn't paid—I don't begrudge them." She was quiet for a minute, and then in a voice very different from the light tone she had used before, she said, "One of the men, Asad, had a rather unhappy tale. His two brothers were conscripted into the Turks' army and were killed in Crete fighting the Greeks."

Edith stopped abruptly, as though she was sorry she had told Asad's story. Looking for a diversion, she picked up my sketch of the white cyclamen and held it to the candlelight. "This is very fine," she said. "I had no idea you had so much talent. I shall certainly make use of it."

I was pleased. "I've never done flowers before."

"All the more amazing. You have a natural talent that we will have to develop. It would be a great help to me to have someone who can sketch the specimens I collect. The rare form of ranunculus that I found today I believe is an entirely new species. One day there may be a *Ranunculus phillipsus* named for me, and you shall sketch it. Together, Julia, we will make an excellent pair. I must say you are the one person whose company I enjoy on this tour, for you are the only one who is not greedy for something. Now I'm for a few hours' sleep."

Edith, however, woke frequently, and I could hear her tossing about. "Are you upset over what happened?" I asked.

"No, no," Edith said. "It's the lice that I picked up lounging about in their tent. Tomorrow I shall have a good bath and a sprinkling with my Keating's powder. We must tell Habib to be sure to keep my sheets separate from the others."

The mukari were careless with the sheets, and a few days later I had lice.

X

KARYATEIN

I WAS AWAKENED BY the muezzin—the crier who summons the faithful to prayer—as he started his five-times-a-day ritual. Edith, who must have been tired from her adventures and her sleepless night, remained asleep. On a suitcase next to her bed lay her glasses, neatly folded on a copy of the Koran. She told me she read a sura, a chapter, from it each evening. Monsieur Louvois had admired the book with its tooled leather cover. "Very rare," he said. "Sixteenth century. Perhaps you would care to sell it?"

Edith had responded indignantly. "No. Must you lay your hands on everything you see?"

The Koran's cover was decorated with cruelly beaked birds hidden in leafy trees and tigers springing out of a bank of flowers onto the backs of terrified gazelles. "The Koran is more than the Arab religion," she had told me. "It's their survival as a people. The Arab language is forbidden in the Turkish courts and in all official Turkish offices. If an Arab wishes to govern his own people, he must do so in the language of the Turks. That is why the Arabs cling to their Koran. As long as they know it chapter and verse, they keep their language and their identity as well."

While the muezzin called and Edith slept on, I reached for my slippers, shaking each one as Edith had taught me, lest it harbor a scorpion. Pattering over to the tent flap, I pushed aside the flap to see the mukaris praying, their robes and kaffiyehs falling forward and winging back with their devotions. The sun was already blazing, and I knew the day would be hot.

His prayers over, Mastur brought a jug of washing water, which he delivered with a tender smile and modest, downcast eyes, his long lashes fluttering at me in a saucy way. *"Moyêh,"* he said, and grinned. He pronounced the word meaning "water" with an almost worshipful tone and a smile on his face.

I was eager to see Graham and hurried into my clothes, modestly slipping my underwear on under the cover of my nightgown. Edith, who was now awake and chattering about the specimens she had discovered the evening before, pulled her nightgown over her head without a blush, exposing her sagging flesh, which she proceeded to splash with water in the racketing manner of a bathing bird.

"It is somehow a very great treat to come upon flowers in the desert, a kind of gift given by someone who can least afford it," she said. She was pulling on a faded pink undershirt and knickers. "Louvois is right. The real excitement is in finding something for which you haven't been looking—finding, as he would say, the *'singulier.'* There is a great difference between those who want to see only what they understand and those who are willing to be surprised by a miracle."

I was flattered by Edith's pronouncements and lectures, for I understood that she liked me and was eager to pass on to me some of the many things she had learned in her travels.

Breakfast was simple: hard-boiled eggs, dates and figs, a melon, and flatbread still warm from the coals. Graham and I helped each other. I neatly peeled his egg for him, and he slathered honey on my bread, licking his fingers afterward. Mastur handed around tiny cups of dark, rich coffee spiced with a few grains of aromatic cardamom. In the past Mastur had appeared to be closest to Edith, but now, to my surprise, he seemed to have taken a special liking to Father, for he made a point of serving Father first and with great deference. The moment breakfast was finished, everything was whisked away and packed.

We were a cheerful lot that morning. Monsieur Louvois, who had appeared in a silk kaffiyeh, was teased mercilessly. Graham asked, "I suppose in that getup you'll want to ride the camel today?"

Monsieur Louvois always enjoyed being the center of attention, and when it was time to leave, he approached the couched camel, which was slobbering over its cud, and tried to clamber on it as if he were scaling a wall. Father would have nothing to do with the antics, but the mukaris emitted peals of laughter at his awkwardness. Hakki stood by, embarrassed that one of his charges should willingly appear so foolish. I was sure he felt it reflected badly on his own dignity.

Our caravan followed the wadi between bleak hills to a small village, where after suitable baksheesh was paid, water was taken on from the town well. Near the well was an ancient castle, its tower and some of its crumbling walls decorated with the Maltese crosses of the crusaders.

"Why would crusaders willingly leave the green island of England for this godforsaken outpost?" Father asked no one in particular. He had been looking weary, and I thought his question reflected something of his own feelings.

Unlike my father, I was growing to love the desert more each day. Years of the dull life I had lived disappeared, until all that was left of my mind was a clean emptiness. I was becoming accustomed to Fadda's gait and gave myself over to the little horse's movements. Fadda picked her way gracefully over the stones, leaving me to think my own thoughts of how far I had traveled and how eager I was to see what surprises further travel would bring.

Graham interrupted my thoughts to point out a patch of sky where bright blue was giving way to a sulfurous yellow. "What is it?" I asked, only mildly curious, considering it another display set forth by the desert for my amusement.

"I'm afraid it might mean a storm, and a bad one."

"It rains in the desert?"

"Yes, and like all things in the desert, the rains are unusually harsh."

Abdullah was already signaling the caravan to stop. The horses sensed the storm; shivering and tugging at their reins, they were made secure, then we riders huddled together while the sky darkened and the wind rushed through the slot of the wadi. Abdullah shooed us out of the wadi's dry river course, for though it was dry now, rainwater would soon come surging through it.

We grabbed whatever protection we could find. Hats were pulled down and jacket collars turned up. Hakki threw saddle blankets at everyone and implored us to stay together.

Only the camel, having changed itself into a boulder, was indifferent to the approaching storm.

At a little distance Abdullah and the mukaris gathered their robes around them, transforming themselves into shapeless black humps. Graham joined them and crouched next to Mohammed, with whom he quietly carried on an intense conversation.

Edith made a tent of her blanket and used the halt to jot some notes, continually losing bits of paper to the gale. Monsieur Louvois, looking put out, as if the storm were some trial sent solely for his torment, hunched himself into as small a target as possible. Father pulled me down next to him. The rough texture of his tweed jacket and the familiar smell of tobacco sent me back to some unremembered sheltering in my childhood.

"You won't like this," he said. "It's not like London, where you can escape a little shower by running into the nearest tea shop." I felt a splash on my hand and another on my face. The next moment the wind snatched away my hat and tugged at my clothes. A cloud of brown dust flew up at the same moment that a wall of water slammed into us. I could barely see my father, who was only inches away. The rain poured down, drenching us until we were sodden sponges. Water careened over the hills that edged the wadi, puddling among the rocks and pebbles, creating rivulets that swelled into sluices, filling the wadi with a torrent of water. My hair had blown loose and was plastered in wet rags against my face. My jacket and skirt clung to me, smothering like a second, damp skin.

The mukaris cursed while the camel made a kind of coughing noise and the horses whinnied and neighed their complaints. Worst of all were the winds, which lifted the sand and dust so the rain was a brew of silt congealing into a mucky slime on our wet faces and clothes. When the rain finally stopped and we saw one another, our alarm and misery dissolved into laughter.

Graham said, "We look like prehistoric creatures climbing out of the primordial mud."

"Something of a nuisance," Edith said, "but most welcome. One rain like this will grow flowers for years to come."

We begged Abdullah for water to wash in, but he refused, warning, "There is no water between here and Karyatein. We mustn't waste what we have." He pointed to the puddles. "You may wash with that, but do not drink it."

Graham soaked his handkerchief in the water and, tilting up my chin with his hand, began to scrub my face. Laughing, I reached up and did the same for him while

Father scowled at our foolishness. The coolness of the water was pleasant, and Monsieur Louvois, seeing the camel drinking, put a little of it in his mouth, only to spit it out. Abdullah, watching him, laughed; nothing pleased him more than one of us making a fool of himself. "How can it rain salt water?" Louvois asked.

"The hills are of salt," Abdullah said. "The rain carries salt with it. To the camel it makes no difference."

We were a ragged group coming into Karyatein, but the villagers were too busy repairing the damage the rain had done to their homes and tents to bother with us. Only the children took notice, running alongside our horses and laughing at how we looked. Karyatein was a nondescript jumble of white blockhouses surrounded by Bedouin tents woven from black goat hair. Camp was set up at the edge of the village, and each of us was given a basinful of water to clean up. Toward the end of our washing, the water was thick mud. It was Mohammed who saved us by learning from the villagers that a small stream ran through the village.

Edith and I were given the privilege of bathing first, while the men, well away from the stream, stood with their backs turned to us to preserve our modesty against a knot of curious children. The stream was lukewarm and little more than a trickle; worse yet, while walking down to its bank, Edith and I saw the camel urinating into the water, its head held up in a kind of offhand ecstasy, but the water appeared clear and in our grubbiness we didn't care. Before the men had their turn, we changed into clean clothes, Edith borrowing a robe from Mastur.

Mastur had managed to shoot some rock partridges, and Edith in a fit of enthusiasm went off looking for wild asparagus while Hakki stared after her, fretting. Father oversaw the cooking of the birds, and Edith returned with a bag of small green spears and a handful of wild garlic. Monsieur Louvois had discovered there was a local wine. Although the Arabs do not drink, Karyatein had vineyards.

Monsieur Louvois said, "They appear not to care about the corruption of infidels, and send their wine on with traders traveling to Damascus."

Hakki, happy to see us all getting along, beamed at us like a parent whose children are enjoying themselves in a harmless way. It was Monsieur Louvois who ended Hakki's pleasure by asking him where he had taught school.

"In Damascus."

"What kind of school was it?" Everyone listened politely to Monsieur Louvois's questions and Hakki's answers.

"It was just a special school of no particular importance."

129

"It was for special students, *n'est-ce pas?*"

"In a way." Hakki was growing uncomfortable.

Monsieur Louvois persisted. "What kind of special students?"

Hakki was goaded into the truth. "They were the sons of soldiers," he mumbled.

"You were an *employé* of the Turkish military?"

"Only to teach their children," Hakki insisted, but Monsieur Louvois, Father, and Graham were all looking at Hakki in an odd way. Only Edith appeared unsurprised. After a bit everyone went back to eating and the banter died out, but I could see the men had become suspicious of Hakki's relationship with the Turkish army.

The tents were pitched within sight of the town, and all during dinner we heard eerie music, its notes drawn out as though they were being pulled endlessly through some musical knothole. Interspersed with the music were shouts and laughter. When we questioned Abdullah, he said, "The daughter of the local sheikh, the head of this tribe, has just been married, and the village will celebrate for three days."

With no thought that my wish would be taken seriously, I said, "I'd have given anything to see that celebration."

Abdullah bowed in my direction and went jogging off in

the direction of the music. A few minutes later he returned with the father of the bride, a short, squat man with a moon face and eyes that were all over us. He bowed obsequiously, and Abdullah translated the man's cordial invitation for us to "bring honor to my humble house."

The more he groveled, the more we were sure he did not want us, but it was too late to refuse. The irony did not escape Father. "We irritate him if we come and insult him if we don't."

Monsieur Louvois said, "We must bring a *cadeau*, some little gift. Money?"

"Money would insult him further," Edith said, and Father agreed.

"What about this?" I held up a small silver case. "I haven't powdered my nose since we left Beirut."

"Just the thing," Edith said. "She can keep her henna in it." Edith turned to me, explaining, "Henna is a reddish-orange powder the women put on their faces and hands to enhance their beauty, rather in the way an Englishwoman might use rouge."

The father of the bride sent one of his sons, a slim, handsome boy with glistening oiled hair and a friendly manner, to escort us. Only Father stayed behind. "I have been to more wedding receptions than I care to recall, and I am sure one is much like another."

The entire village was crowded into a courtyard over which a huge tent had been erected. The tent was illuminated by torches casting eerie shadows.

Everything was revealed slowly in the dim light; handsome rugs and cushioned banquettes, and in the center of the tent long boards supported by trestles and spread with embroidered cloths. On these improvised tables were dishes of pickled aubergine and boiled eggs, brass trays heaped with fresh and dried fruits, and enormous bowls of rice and mutton kept warm on braziers. Pastries oozing a gooey mix of almonds and honey were arranged in pretty patterns on palm fronds. As our little company walked into the tent, there was a sudden silence, but almost at once the music and laughter resumed; even the sight of a band of exotic foreigners—a young Turk, an older woman dressed in the robe of an Arab, and an English girl who kept looking at a man with hair the color of fire—could not squelch their enthusiasm.

The tent was divided by a light curtain. The men were gathered on one side of the tent, wearing white robes. Some wore the fez, others the kaffiyeh. They shouted back and forth to one another, their voices rough and boisterous, their laughter bawdy. At their center was the groom, in a white robe and a white kaffiyeh tied with a gold cord. His robe was too large for him, and he walked with a swagger. Looking closely at him, I saw that he had no beard.

Giggles and trills of pleasure came from the other side of the tent, where the women were circling a dais in a measured dance. They were dressed in brightly colored burkas. Their faces, except for their heavily kohled eyes, were veiled. On the dais was seated the bride, who we were told had to remain on view as a kind of ornament throughout the three-day celebration. She was enveloped in colored shawls and bedecked with gold bracelets, earrings, and nose ring. An intricate design was picked out in indigo dye on the skin of her neck, and the palms of her hands were hennaed. A crown, slightly askew, was on her head. Like the groom, she seemed a child got up in a costume for some school play.

Monsieur Louvois and the other men gravitated to the men's half of the tent, while I entered on the women's side to give the silver case to the bride. She looked up at a stout woman hung with bangles for permission to accept the present. The woman nodded, her bangles tinkling with assent. Only then did the girl allow herself to take the case into her hands and examine it, which she did with pleasure. I showed her how it opened, and she cried out with delight at the surprise of a mirror inside.

After a bit I left the women's side and found Graham waiting for me. "How old do you think the bride is?" I asked.

"Not more than thirteen, perhaps younger."

"But that's terrible. How can she know her own mind at that age?"

"There is no need for her to know her mind; her father will have made the choice for her, and this will be her first glimpse of her husband."

"But that's barbarous." I was shocked.

Graham smiled. "You can't pretend marriages in our country are not arranged with an eye to class and money."

"But at least the principals know each other," I protested.

"And how many truly happy marriages have you witnessed in our country?"

I laughed. "You're too cynical. I think it's a show you put on."

Smiling, he said, "What does it matter how the marriage turns out if the wedding is an occasion for pleasure?"

We stood together in the darkness, watching the festivities in the divided tent. The men danced, the silver and brass handles of the daggers they held aloft reflecting the light from the torches. I had never seen men dance together, and it had a strange effect upon me. I turned to look for Graham, wanting him next to me, but he was gone. One of the men smiled at me, catching my eye each time he whirled around.

The man's smile now became a hungry leer. I moved quickly into the safety of the women's side. The young girls were clustered together in a corner, giggling behind their veils. Only the older women danced. They moved more slowly and more circumspectly than the men, but the slowness that at first seemed stately became provocative, and the swaying women looked naked in their robes.

The music became louder and louder until my ears were ringing. The torches and braziers threw off so much heat in the crowded tent that it grew stifling. I slipped out for some air and, walking a short distance from the celebration, fell at once into the emptiness of the desert. In London I rarely saw the stars, and then only the bright ones. In the desert the sky was populated with countless stars and looked like a great black tent pricked all over to let in the light of some night sun.

Drawn into the desert's silence, I wandered a distance from the tent until I heard voices talking together so softly that I was sure the words were meant only for the two speakers. The voices came from two figures in the shadows of a cluster of huts. I recognized the sound of Graham's voice. The other man was Mohammed.

I heard Mohammed say, "There is nothing to be done here. This sheikh will not hear of the Young Turks; to him all Turks are evil and will never change their ways. This sheikh prefers to play a game of intrigue with Britain and France, but he is a fool if he believes Britain and France will do something for his people. In Palmyra I will take you to many tribes that will welcome the revolution of your Young Turks." Mohammed, suddenly aware of my presence, melded with the shadows and disappeared. Graham came up to me and, grabbing my arm roughly, said in an accusing voice, "I thought you were with the others."

"I could say the same."

His hand was hurting my arm. I pulled away.

"I'm sorry," he said. "I've grown to suspect everyone."

"Why should you suspect anyone?"

"I can't tell you that. I can only ask you to trust me and to promise not to repeat anything you might have overheard."

"You are always asking me to keep your secrets, but you won't confide in me."

"I'll ask something more of you: that you say you and I wandered away from the wedding together. It isn't for my sake that I ask it but for Mohammed's. He is taking a risk in associating himself with my cause."

"What kind of risk? And what kind of cause?"

"No more questions. Later, perhaps. Will you promise?"

I nodded and then, realizing he could not see me in the darkness, said, "Yes."

His voice was suddenly chilling. "Why are you out here? Perhaps your father sent you. I gave him my word not to reveal his identity, but I won't have him spying on me."

"How can you suggest something like that? I'm not to ask questions of you, but you may ask questions of me?"

His voice softened, and he took my face between his hands. "Julia, I trusted you at the café in Damascus and I promise to tell you the rest later."

When we heard someone approaching, Graham hastily kissed my forehead and moved away from me. Edith frowned when she saw me with Graham, but all she said was "You two missed a delightful speech by the father of the bride honoring his new son-in-law. The same speech might have been given in any English city—Newcastle or Stoke-on-Trent."

At the camp we found Father and the dragoman, Abdullah, talking together, Father in a camp chair, Abdullah squatting next to him. They drew apart, Abdullah making a pretense of feeding thorn branches into the fire and Father leaning back in his camp chair. They had the air of conspirators. Graham looked at me reproachfully, as if to say, "You see, your father has his own secrets."

Later that night I lay awake listening to the tent creak and whisper in the wind. I knew my father was on a mission for the Foreign Office and that Graham had some plan of a revolution by the Young Turks against the sultan. I longed to be caught up in my father's and Graham's worlds of conspiracy and passion. At the same time, I was put off by their greediness for land and souls that did not belong to them. I was suspicious of Father's involving Abdullah and of Graham's involving Mohammed in their schemes. Even Edith seemed to have a secret relationship with Mastur. I felt as if I were in the middle of some dangerous conspiracy and at any moment something might happen that would change all our lives.

I was just drifting off when I heard a bloodcurdling shriek. Edith sprang out of her bed and, grabbing her robe, ran from the tent. Afraid Graham might be in some danger, I followed her. The screams were coming from Habib, who was rolling over and over on the ground, his face contorted. Graham, in a flannel robe, his hair tousled, was holding up a lantern while Abdullah tried to restrain Habib.

Father strode up wearing his oilskin over his pajamas.

The green-and-white-striped pajamas were familiar to me. I had taken them from the laundress and placed them in my father's dressing room dozens of times. Seeing them now made me feel for a moment that I was back home in Durham Place and had run into my father on the staircase or along a hall. Then I remembered Habib writhing on the ground.

"What is happening here?" Father demanded as if he were a commanding officer faced with soldiers who had started a battle without his permission.

"Habib has been bitten by a snake," Graham said. "He was sleeping on the ground, and the snake must have crept close to him for warmth. When the poor fellow got up to relieve himself, the snake bit him."

Edith hurried at once to Habib. "Listen to me!" she commanded. "What kind of snake was it? Tell us at once."

"A viper! A viper!" Habib wailed, and began to moan that he was dying.

Edith dashed off and returned a moment later with a knife. "Get someone to help you hold him down," she told Abdullah. "I must cut his wound and suck out the poison."

"Never! I will not be sliced with a *sikkîn*! I would rather die!" Habib cried.

Abdullah called Mastur to help him, but Mastur shook

his head. *"Insulata,"* he said. "It is willed that he die. There is no need to send him to Allah in pieces."

In the midst of this Monsieur Louvois appeared, got up in a silk paisley dressing gown complete with ascot. He walked nonchalantly into the circle of light as though he were entering a drawing room. Father shoved the lantern into Monsieur Louvois's unwilling hand and knelt down to grip Habib. Edith was leaning over the terrified man with her knife.

"Do you know what you are doing?" Father demanded.

"Certainly," she said shortly. She made two deep cuts in Habib's leg in the shape of a cross, and when the blood began oozing out, she leaned over and sucked at the leg, spitting out the blood and venom. I was at once sickened and fascinated, wanting and not wanting to look. In the light of the lantern, the scene of the terrified man, now submissive with fright, and Edith leaning over him to clean out his wound, made me long for pencil and paper.

Father handed Edith a flask of brandy and told her to rinse her mouth with it. "You were rather efficient at that operation," he said.

Edith spat out the first gulp of brandy and swallowed the second. "I sincerely hope this doesn't mean you will all consider me some sort of nurse and come to me about your sick tummies and constipation."

Mastur helped Abdullah carry a trembling Habib away. There was a complicit smile on Mastur's face as he murmured to Edith, "Now at last you have an Arab blood brother."

XI

PALMYRA

Miss Julia Hamilton
Palmyra, Syria
April 10, 1907

Mrs. Edgar Hamilton
77 South Audley Street
London, England

Dear Aunt Harriet,

I have no idea when this letter will be mailed, but I must get down my impressions of Palmyra while they are still fresh, for it's a magical city, worth the arduous trip and the lice. Yes, your dear Julia has lice! Never fear, I shall leave them all here in the desert.

King Solomon built Palmyra in the wilderness, and Mark Antony loved the city. Queen Zenobia, who once ruled the city, was carried back to Rome in chains of gold.

Chains of gold! *It takes my breath away. That is just how I feel when I see the city—breathless, not so much with what is here as what was once here.*

The Temple of the Sun is visible from a long distance, for it is raised on a hill, but few of the rooms have more than one wall, and all one sees between the columns is blue sky. All these glories were built with a limestone that is the rosy color of the inside of a seashell, so for all the cold message of destruction, the ruins still glow warmly in the sun.

Sometimes I feel the Julia who lived in Durham Place is still back there in England, wandering alone and bored through that great empty house, while a new Julia wanders on horseback through a desert with fascinating companions and has one amazing adventure after another. How sorry I feel for that first girl.

> *Your loving niece,*
> *Julia*

It was true that I was having adventures and seeing a magical city, but I was also feeling a little useless. Father was carrying out some secret business for the Foreign Office; Edith was searching out rare plants, and Monsieur Louvois rare antiques; and Graham was involved in some grand plot;

while I was only an onlooker. "Perhaps," I thought, "I'll find some purpose in Palmyra."

We rode into Palmyra on the Muslim Day of the Dead. After hours of barren stretches and miles of stone and sand, Palmyra with its ruined temples appeared more illusion than reality. As we entered the city, the first thing we saw was the burial ground, where Arab women were garnishing the graves with wilting nosegays of wild irises and hyacinths laced with branches of almond. It would have been a mournful scene except for the small children who frolicked among the graves like puppy dogs. "I don't know why the dead are always left to the care of women," Edith said. "I suppose it is the logical progression from birth." She left me for a moment to talk with the women and examine their flowers for some blossom or bud not in her collection.

In Palmyra we all found something. The sheikh from Karyatein had sent a message to the local sheikh in Palmyra introducing our party. Father took advantage of this to request an invitation to the sheikh's home.

"I am eager to meet the man," he said, but a moment later I saw him sink into a chair as if he had been overtaken by a wave of dizziness. I was concerned, for I had noticed in the last few days that he tired easily and was eating very little. I begged him to rest, but he soon recovered and insisted on the visit.

"Julia," he said to me, "while I have you alone, I must ask you to spend less time with Geddes. I am growing more and more wary of the man. I consider his politics bizarre. What possible reason can an Englishman find for enlisting in the cause of the Young Turks' revolution?"

"I don't have anything to do with his politics," I said, and felt guilty, for that was not strictly true.

"Nevertheless, I foresee in him nothing but trouble." After a half hour's rest Father made his way to the sheikh's home. I supposed he meant to court him for England with a message of friendship and vague promises.

I ignored Father's request and allowed Graham to take me away to wander among the ruined temples. "Everyone on the tour seems to know exactly what they want," I said. "I wish I had some sort of purpose instead of just following everyone about."

"You might start by tying up that father of yours. He'll promise the sheikh that England will be a friend to the Arab, when all he wants is for England to get a foothold here." Graham saw that I was offended, and apologized. "It's foolish to discuss politics on an afternoon like this. What I want is to be alone with you."

We wandered hand in hand through what had been the marketplace. "I read that tigers and slave girls were sold here," I said.

"And gold and spices."

"Elephants and peacocks."

From the marketplace we entered one of the funerary towers where the ancient Palmyrans were buried. It was an eerie place; we came upon ghostly bits of bone and tatters of winding sheets and in one tomb a fragment of a mummy.

I was anxious to hurry away. Returning to the camp, we passed through the village, where the few inhabitants lived. There could not have been more than forty or fifty huts. At first glance the huts seemed small and mean. I looked more closely.

"Graham, that hut has a marble frieze for one of its walls," I said. The frieze was made from the same rosy limestone as the temple. The carving on the frieze was of an eagle, its wings outspread, its claws curved to grasp some unseen prey.

"Over there." Graham pointed to where a gracefully grooved column supported the disintegrating tin roof of a shed.

The huts, which had appeared merely ramshackle at first, were put together with magnificent architectural fragments reclaimed from the ancient city. The hovels were like beggars whose clothes had been patched with the castoffs of kings.

I asked, "How can you risk your life for a cause when you see how nations fall apart? Do you really believe people are wiser now than they were a thousand years ago?"

"Of course not. I'm not a Utopian. My goals are much more modest: I merely believe things could be a little better—or perhaps it's the risk itself that attracts me." He laughed. "It may be that I am a born meddler."

I wasn't interested in choosing sides. I only wanted to spend time with Graham. I did not want the trip to end. I did not want to go back to a world without Graham. I clung more tightly to his hand, as if I could keep him by my side by sheer force. He must have guessed my feelings, for he choose a path that concealed us from curious eyes. The path wandered through an old orchard of ancient apricot and pomegranate trees. The apricot trees were in bloom, and as Graham took me in his arms, the blossoms in the lightest of breezes detached themselves from the branches and fell over us like fragrant snow.

That afternoon Graham rode off with Mohammed. The two of them were gone for hours, returning hot and dusty from a direction that suggested nothing but emptiness, leaving me to wonder what mystery they had been up to.

During Graham's absence Monsieur Louvois had called to me, "For your eyes only. You are an *artiste* and will appreciate it." Word of his gold must have traveled from Jerud to the Bedouin tribes near Palmyra, for a steady flow of Bedouin came and went with ancient bits and pieces to sell to him. The object he held out, enfolded in a square of worn blue cotton, made me catch my breath. It was a winged ibex, a magical antelope, no larger than my little finger and made of silver with gold splashed on its face and wings. I couldn't guess at the value of the piece, but the graceful curve of the horns, the supple grace of the body, the frightened look on its face, and the impression that it was about to leap to freedom gave it a haunting beauty.

"It's magnificent," I whispered.

"Achaemenian, perhaps twenty-five hundred years old. You can have your grand Greek sculptures; I prefer something the hand can close over. This could hold its own against a Michelangelo."

"Where do the Bedouin find such things?"

"They have learned from the professional archaeologists who hire their people to work in the digs. The archaeologists excavate one site while the Bedouin find a site for themselves nearby. Unhappily, they are not as careful as the archaeologists."

"If there is damage done, don't you feel responsible when the loot is being sold to you?"

Monsieur Louvois looked offended and plucked the ibex from my hand. "Loot? *Le butin*, not a pretty word. These men mean to sell, and if I do not buy, someone else will, and the someone else may have no idea of beauty and value. At least I will see that this finds a proper home and is preserved."

"How will you bear to part with it?" I asked, already missing its small weight in my hand.

"As for that, we shall see."

"Won't you risk imprisonment by taking it out of the country?" He merely smiled, but I knew he would take the risk gladly.

Edith's specimen cases were rapidly filling. I sometimes tagged along with her, making sketches and watercolors of her finds. I had developed a trick of setting white flowers against their green leaves rather than against the white paper, where they had to be strongly outlined to set them off.

"An ingenious idea," Edith said. "Look at how it shows off the veining in this tulip." Edith knelt by the flower I had painted. She regarded it with the same tenderness that Monsieur Louvois had shown his ibex, but a moment later she had clipped off the bloom to squash in her press and was digging for its bulb.

"How can you say it is so beautiful and then let it die like that?"

"Don't think of its death but of its resurrection," Edith said. "The flower dies, but the bulb lives to produce more flowers and more bulbs in a place where many people will enjoy it. If you and I had not been here, this flower would have been seen by no more than a handful of desert wanderers."

I thought it was Monsieur Louvois's argument all over again. Later she found a scarlet anemone. "You know the story, don't you?" Edith asked. "Aphrodite loved Adonis, but because he was a mortal, she could not prevent a wild boar from killing him. She caused a red anemone to grow wherever a drop of his blood fell."

"Do you travel to look for flowers or do you look for flowers so that you can travel?" I asked her.

Edith made a dismissive gesture. "I am here merely to do a job for the Royal Botanic Gardens at Kew. I have no designs on the country." She gave me a long look. "Because I am fond of you and trust you, I will tell you a story I have told to very few." Though no one was near, she lowered her voice. "When I was eleven, a terrifying thing happened to me. I was living in northern India in the town of Meerut. My father was in the British civil service. My childhood was a free one. Except in church, I ran about barefoot. We lived a little outside the English settlement, which was remarked upon by the English residents, but my mother loved the countryside and avoided the English teas and dinner parties of the Raj, the English rulers of India. The house for me was only for meals and sleep. My ayah, my nursemaid, was a young girl who was content to sit on the riverbank with me, our toes cooling in the water, watching kingfishers arrow down from a tree branch to snatch a silver fish.

"England was busy in those days sweeping up one Hindu state after another. They concocted a clever scheme. If a ruler died without an heir, England got his state as a prize. The English tidied up and organized India, bringing their customs, their religion, their air of superiority. All the while the Indians were growing more and more resentful. When their resentment boiled over, my parents were dead, killed with the other English by an uprising of the sepoys, the very soldiers the English had trained to protect them.

"I was shipped back to England, the country whose greed had taken away my parents. I was cared for by a joyless aunt who kept me in tightly laced kid boots and starched blouses that scratched. The moment I had the chance, I chose sun and distance, and I never looked back.

My return trips to England, and Kew in particular, are rare and brief. I feel as strange in London as I feel at home in the desert."

"Edith, how terrible that must have been for you. I am so sorry."

"It was a long time ago, Julia, but I recall it as if it were yesterday."

"Yet in spite of the horrible way your parents died, you seem more on the side of the Indians than the British."

"I learned early in life what evil can come from the sins of empire. I am not here as your father is or as Geddes is or even Louvois. They are like guests in a house they mean to rob. Someday this country will be freed of the Turks and returned to the Arabs, and I say it can't be soon enough." Watching her stab her trowel furiously into the earth to pry out another flower, I shuddered at Edith's anger.

Later that day, as Monsieur Louvois, Graham, and I were having tea, Father, dressed carefully in a clean field jacket and trousers and a slouch hat, left for a second visit with the sheikh. Abdullah, who accompanied him, was also dressed for the occasion and wore a black-striped robe with a black kaffiyeh wrapped with a gold cord. They disappeared into the afternoon haze, from which the columns of the ancient city seemed to grow like stone trees.

Monsieur Louvois regarded Father's departure with a rising irritation. "I tried to see the sheikh all day yesterday," he said. "He must be *insensé* if he believes the British will do something for him. It is we, the French, who understand the Arabs."

"I didn't know you took an interest in politics," Graham said.

Flustered, Monsieur Louvois responded, "My visit was not intended as politics; only as a polite gesture."

"Actually, I'm rather pleased Hamilton is seeing the sheikh," Graham said. "Perhaps he'll learn what's going on in this village. Something unpleasant, I'm sure. The villagers won't look us in the eye and disappear around corners. Doors and tent flaps close when we approach. We seem to have come at an inconvenient time."

But when he returned, Father had little to say. He spoke pleasantly of his visit with the sheikh. "The sheikh is an educated man. He not only speaks English but also knows his Latin." He turned to me. "I asked if I might bring you along on my next visit, Julia. He said the women would be honored."

The home of the sheikh was set apart from the rest of the village, and the next day Father and I made our way up a steep rise to a hilltop on which was balanced a tumble of sun-blanched boxlike structures. I noticed that Father had to stop several times to catch his breath, and on the steepest part of the path he had even taken my arm. His needing my support gave me a strange feeling, as if the world were upside down, but when I asked if he was well, he brushed aside my question. "Perfectly well, just a bit of tummy trouble."

There was nothing green to soften the sharp edges of the houses, only a few dying almond trees. Hangers-on lounged outside the entrance of the largest structure, watching our arrival, suspicious looks on their faces.

"They don't like us, do they?" I asked Father.

"It isn't a matter of 'liking.' They find me suspect, for I ask questions. Unlike Geddes, however, I do not tell them what they ought to do, and for that they give me credit."

"What questions do you ask?"

"I suppose you may as well know what I'm up to. Graham knows, I'm sure, and it isn't all that dramatic. I am merely trying to get some idea of how friendly the Arab sheikhs in these remote villages are to Britain, but none of that involves you, so you must put it out of your mind. This afternoon we are merely making a social visit, and everything will be most friendly even though you will appear to them as very strange indeed."

"What do you mean?"

"A woman wearing clothes like yours, walking about wherever you please—that is not understood."

"But what about Edith? She often travels alone through Arab country more remote than this, and the Arabs seem to accept her."

"The Arabs see Edith not as a woman but as a phenomenon. Should she be making the visit you and I are making, she would be expected to spend her time with the sheikh, not with his harem. Still, you needn't worry; the more outlandish they find you, the more courteous they will be."

I looked forward to the visit and to seeing what life was like for the women, and wondered how it would compare with my own protected and limited life. I suspected the Julia Hamilton of Durham Place might have much in common with the women shut up in the harem.

As we reached the entrance to the sheikh's house, the small band of men who had been squatting there stood and bowed stiffly to us, keeping their eyes from me, the way you might try not to stare at a person with an embarrassing affliction. Father rapped lightly on the door with the iron knocker.

"*Mîn?*"

"Carlton Hamilton." We heard a scuffling inside, followed by footsteps. The sheikh himself opened the door and greeted us, then led us into a reception room. A platformlike divan, covered with richly colored carpets, ran along three walls of the room. Everything was spare. There were small brass tables and a carved chest bound in iron.

The sheikh was tall and gaunt, the flesh carved from his cheeks and body, but there was no feeling of frailty; on the contrary, his lean build suggested a man who had put everything aside, the better to do battle. He held his hands folded tightly in front of him as if he feared I might make some impulsive gesture, perhaps attempt to shake his hand. I was sure physical contact with a woman would try his courtesy beyond its limits.

He led us across a courtyard where withered plants leaned hopelessly toward a dry fountain. A few empty tin cans were scattered about, and a goat with opalescent yellow eyes and a beard like the sheikh's was tethered to a stake. The sheikh's tone was ingratiating as he told me, "From first light the women of my household have not ceased making preparations for your coming."

"I am sorry to give so much trouble," I said.

"There is no trouble, only honor. My oldest sister, Fatima, has a few words of English. As children we lived in

Damascus for some years. My father sold saddles there that our tribe and our neighboring tribes have made for many centuries. I was sent to St. Paul's School, run by the British Syrian Mission, where I studied English. My sister benefited from my knowledge, for I would come home from school each day and give her all my new English words to play with. But I have chattered on enough. Let my servant take you to the women's quarter before the women collapse altogether from anticipation."

I followed the servant, whose obsequiousness only underlined his distaste for me. The windows that gave out onto the court were grilled, but shadowed movements behind the lattices suggested I was being watched.

The servant knocked on a door, and then with a deep bow he hastily left me, as if the room might contain some dreaded disease. After a moment or two the door was opened by a tall woman whom I took to be Fatima. She was thin, like her brother, the sheikh, with a body slimmer than that of the other women. She was handsomely robed in a turquoise caftan embroidered in gold thread with a matching veil. All that was visible of her were her dark eyes, which were heavily outlined in kohl. I could tell little from the disembodied eyes; I decided that all the tales of "expressive eyes" were poetic nonsense. Instead I took my cue from the woman's voice, a voice controlled and cordial, with a practiced firmness suggesting patience that had been sorely tried but not exhausted.

"It should be my sister-in-law Alia's honor to greet you, but because she has no English, she has kindly allowed me the privilege." The sheikh's wife, a smaller woman with soft curves, stood beside Fatima. Alia uttered a few encouraging-sounding words of Arabic and indicated, with a gesture that set a dozen gold arm bangles clattering, that I was to enter the room. *"Kêf hâlik?"* she added.

It was an inquiry that always followed a greeting. I had heard it a hundred times on the trip: "How is your health?" I managed the appropriate answer: *"El-hamdu lillâh, taiyib,"* meaning "Well, thank God"; this elicited giggles of pleasure and surprise that I should know even that small bit of their language.

Though little light entered the room through the latticed windows, I had an almost dizzying impression of pattern and color. The walls of the room were hung with striped draperies, and the floors were covered with patterned Turkish rugs and embroidered cushions. Seated on the cushions were a half dozen women in richly colored robes and veils. Running and tumbling among them was a brood of small children. In a friendly gesture, Fatima and

Alia removed their veils, as did the other women in the room.

Impulsively I said, "How I would love to paint this room with all of you in it."

Fatima sighed. "It is sadness itself to have to refuse you anything, but that would not be allowed. Our images belong to Allah only, praise His name. Any other wish we would be happy to grant you; you have only to ask." The other women did not understand our words, but they followed the inflections in Fatima's voice and now murmured their assent.

In the middle of the room was a low table enameled in blues and greens. Alia knelt at the table, settling her robes in a graceful pool about her, and poured from a doll-size brass coffeepot. Another woman hastened to take up a tiny cup and saucer, and with a graceful bow she served me. The ceremony was solemn until my efforts to settle down onto one of the cushions, while balancing the cup and saucer, caused a wave of tittering that was not so much impolite as encouraging.

Fatima said, "I understand you have come from Damascus. I sometimes think of the streets there. We had a house in the marketplace, so there was much to see when you looked out the windows. Here, at whatever hour you look, there is a sameness."

The sheikh's wife must have interpreted the wistfulness in Fatima's voice as complaint. Frowning, she took up a tray heaped with candied apricots and almonds and thrust them at me with encouraging words, as if to say "How could one be unhappy when there are such tasty things to eat?" The children crowded around me to see what I would choose and to be sure I would not be so greedy as to take what they wanted.

"In our country," I said, "women have a good deal of freedom to go about, but it doesn't lead to much."

"Where would you have it lead?" Fatima asked. "The 'going about,' as you call it, would be freedom enough." The women bent forward to listen to my reply, which was incomprehensible to them but interesting nonetheless.

"What would happen if you did as you wished?" I asked.

Fatima's eyebrows came together in a frown. "I am afraid I have been foolish and misleading in my talk," she said. "What I wish is what all of us wish: to live as my brother asks, for his desires and ours are Allah's." At the sound of Allah's name a little chorus of assent went up around me.

Off to one side I noticed a woman seated by herself. A tear ran down her cheek, leaving a trail of smudged kohl. Seeing my interest in the woman, Fatima hastily attempted to distract me by thrusting a pillow at me, saying, "I understand that you are fond of art. My brother's wife wishes you to see this. It was embroidered by my mother, who was known for her skill."

The pillow depicted a rabbit being pursued by a mountain lion. The animals were full of life, the rabbit sprinting through a field of exquisitely fashioned flowers, the lion about to spring on its prey; the scene caught the menace in a scene that would never come to pass. I turned to Alia and, indicating the cushion, spoke of its beauty, repeating the word *kwaiyis*, meaning "beautiful," a word I had often heard Edith use to describe a flower. The sheikh's wife smiled, and Fatima said they were happy to share something of their culture. More coffee was served, and the tray of apricots and almonds was sent around again.

Fatima translated a question from one of the women about my boots. "She wonders what it feels like to have one's feet so tightly confined."

I unlaced one of the boots and passed it to the woman, who quickly slipped off her sandal and tried to push her foot into the boot. Another woman came to her aid, and there was much giggling and tugging until the boot was forced on and the lacing completed.

I asked Fatima to show me how the veil was worn. At once a veil was brought out from a chest, and the woman wearing my boot draped the soft muslin around me. More laughter and giggles greeted my appearance. I found the material surprisingly easy to breath through, and for a moment, with the veil hiding my face, I was able to ease the rigidly polite expression I wore. I was almost sorry to take the veil off.

The veil was removed and the boot returned. With many thank-yous on my part, and expressions of friendship on the part of Fatima and the other women, I left, noting that when Fatima opened the door, there was no one outside and a servant had to be called to show me out. As I said my farewells, I could not resist trying to take a furtive glance at the woman who had been crying, but the women had replaced their veils and I could not tell them apart.

XII

MORE PALMYRA

H AKKI SURPRISED US AT dinner. "I wonder if you would let me kindly suggest something to you." He smiled nervously at us and continued in a pleading voice. "I think we must leave Palmyra tomorrow, only a day early." That appeared odd to everyone, for we were finding Palmyra agreeable. The weather was mild and the food, because of the local gardens, tasty. For dinner Mastur had just given us aubergine stuffed with tender spring lamb and seasoned with subtle herbs.

Monsieur Louvois spoke of a "rich resource" he had not exhausted. Graham said he had reached a crucial point in his research on the Druzes. Father said nothing, but he was feeling ill again, and I guessed he was not eager to travel.

Hakki persisted. "I promise to find you something of interest near Ain el Beida. I do not want to disturb anyone, but I have learned that something not so nice is about to

163

happen here. The people are impatient for us to leave. The postponement of what is to be done makes them uneasy. It is best we leave as soon as possible."

"What in heaven's name are you talking about?" Edith asked. "Aren't you being a bit presumptuous?" Her tone was not convincing, and I had the uncomfortable feeling that Edith was taking pleasure in goading Hakki and had known all along what he meant, for she spoke the language of the townspeople and was often among them asking questions about herbs and plants.

"What I am trying to tell you," Hakki said in an earnest, embarrassed voice, "is that the sheikh's niece has had something to do with a man other than her husband, and her people do not like it." He appeared angry with us for making him put such a delicate matter into words.

"What do you mean, they don't like it?" Graham asked.

Monsieur Louvois guessed. "There will be a trial followed by a little punishment of some sort, *n'est-ce pas?*"

Hakki said, "The trial has been held, and it will not be a 'little' punishment. The unfortunate man has already been taken care of. The woman is held in the sheikh's house." He dropped his voice so that we could hardly hear the words that followed. "When we leave, there will be a stoning."

I gasped. I saw the weeping woman in the sheikh's

house, the black-stained tears running down her cheek. I was sure it was her. There had been no guard at the door. She might have escaped and hadn't. What did that mean? Was she afraid to make an attempt, or was she resigned to her fate? And which was worse? My hand shook so much, I spilled my coffee.

"Abdullah and the mukaris have known," Hakki went on. "It is just today that I learned. It is terrible. But how is a man to guess at such a thing? And there are those who say we Turks should leave the Arabs to themselves."

Monsieur Louvois, seeing the stricken expression on my face, scolded Hakki. "Look what you have done. You should have kept silent rather than burden us with such news. Even so, I intend to go about my business and forget what I heard. These people will carry on with this *horreur* whether we are here or not."

Father agreed. "These barbarisms have been going on for thousands of years and in one form or another will continue to go on. If one hasn't learned that from the history books, one is dense beyond belief."

"I have a Druze leader coming from a long distance, and he won't be here until tomorrow," Graham said. "I don't see what our leaving will accomplish; in fact, our staying may prolong the unfortunate woman's life and might even lead to some sort of pardon."

In an angry outburst, Edith said, "Instead of playing the part of dense foreigners, why don't you look at the reason behind what is happening? In this world the virtue of the women is crucial to the tribe. Women are held as holy and hence must be blameless. The honor of the family depends on the honor of their women. As to the method, I suggest you cast your minds back to the execution by drawing and quartering that went on in our own enlightened England not all that long ago, or consider the fact that we still have public hangings. In a way this is more humane, for one of her relatives with good aim will end her suffering with the first stone."

I could see the crouching woman, hands held helplessly to her face, waiting. "You are all horrible," I said. My voice was little more than a whisper. Everyone looked at me. "If we do nothing to stop this, we will be murderers as much as they are."

"However you feel about this, Julia," Father said, "hysteria will solve nothing."

"You think only of yourselves." Now my voice was shaking. "You meddle in their affairs and steal things that don't belong to you—the treasures of their ancestors, the very flowers of their fields—but you won't lift a hand to save the poor woman's life."

I turned away in disgust, not thinking of where I was going. When I was a safe distance, I looked back at Palmyra. The shadows created by the lowering sun made the ruins seem alive again. Nothing had changed. There had always been barbarism in that fabled city, and it was there still.

Graham had followed me. He put his arm around my shoulders and said, "Julia, it matters to me what you think. Please listen to what I am trying to do. You are speaking of one life; I am thinking of thousands of lives. The whole Turkish Empire is seething with unrest, and the sultan can't hold it together much longer. The British and French see that. They are plotting to take advantage of Turkey's weakness and partition the country."

"What can you and your Young Turks possibly do against the sultan's forces?"

"Wherever we go, Mohammed and I talk with the leaders of the Druzes. We explain the Young Turk revolution, how the Young Turks will bring democracy to this country, and I urge the Druzes to support the Young Turks. I tell them there will be a revolution followed in Turkey by a constitutional government, with a place in that government for the Arabs."

"Why did you get involved in all this?"

"Why should I merely study history when I can make it? In Damascus, where the Young Turks are very strong, one of their members was able to place Mohammed as a mukari with us. He has been most helpful to me in contacting the local tribesmen. As horrible as that woman's death might be, I can't risk losing the support of the Druze here. They would all be against our interfering in such a matter. You must understand, Julia, there is too much at stake." A moment later he was gone.

I stayed on, listening to the rasping hum of the bees among the pomegranate blossoms, wanting to believe in what Graham was trying to do, telling myself the doomed woman had nothing to do with me; but as much as I cared for Graham, I could not forget the image of the woman. Walking back toward the camp, I saw Edith and confronted her. "You can't really believe we ought to close our eyes to what is happening to that woman?"

Edith shrugged. "What can we do? Even if she could escape, which I doubt, where could she go? No tribe would take her in. You must understand, Julia, that you can't bring your own world with you when you come to a place like this; that is both its blessing and its scourge. One has to admire someone like that woman, who can meet her fate with so much submissiveness."

"I don't see that," I said. "If you are always going to be submissive and resigned, nothing will change." I was speaking of the condemned woman, but I was thinking of myself.

"If you wish to change the world, Julia, don't start with me; it is exactly where you will have the least chance of success."

For the first time, I began to consider the consequences of my visit to the home of the sheikh. I asked Edith, "Will the sheikh be angry because Father and I invited ourselves to his home?"

Edith tried to reassure me. "The sheikh is much too diplomatic to admit to any embarrassment, but I must also tell you: Though the sheikh will say nothing, he doubtless was very put out. He surely knew your father's intentions. Your kind and your countries are forever interfering. One of these days, all of the world will tangle itself in the web of the Levant."

I had wanted to travel, but I had not wanted to come as far as this. I had believed that my travels with Father would be all pleasant adventures. I would travel though Syria, but I would have nothing to do with it. The journey would be for my amusement, like turning pages in a travel book. Instead my whole life was changing. I was forced to think about things I had never cared about or even imagined—a woman's death and the fate of whole countries. I not only had to think about these things, I had to make decisions about them. What I said and what I did suddenly mattered. I had wanted carefree adventure, and now I had responsibility.

Later, when Hakki announced that we would stay one more day and said nothing more about the unfortunate woman, I made no reply.

On our last day in Palmyra, Graham sought me out and, taking my hand, led me to the edge of the ruined city, where a small brook was nothing more than a secret presence snaking along among tall grasses and reeds. As we walked along, little green frogs dappled with gold jumped into the safety of the stream, making plopping sounds that were like musical notes.

I was grateful to Graham, thinking he understood how upset I was and wanted to keep me occupied, but when two figures appeared on horseback, I was suddenly suspicious. My suspicions were confirmed when I heard Graham say, "It's my Druze chieftain, Ismail, come to say farewell, and I see he has another Druze with him." I was sure that Graham had planned to meet the men here, and I wondered if the stroll with me was meant to provide an excuse.

The chieftain and his companion reined in their horses

inches from where Graham and I stood; I felt the pelting of small stones against my legs, making me think again of the condemned woman. Ismail looked at me for a moment, and I could see him deciding, as the owner of the café in Damascus had decided, that I was of no consequence and so he might speak freely in front of me.

"This is the chief from our neighboring tribe," Ismail told Graham.

The companion, a fleshy man with soft cheeks and hands, looked at once hesitant and irritated, as though he were both reluctant and resentful to be there.

"There once was a man, Fakru'd-din Maan," he said to Graham, "who built one of the great houses here in the days when this was an exalted city. Fakru'd-din Maan received tribute from every trader up and down the Syrian coast. He was a rich and happy man until he plotted against the sultan and had to flee for his life. The sultan hunted him down and killed him. Now you ask me to plot against another sultan. Why should I repeat the mistakes of that unwise man, who has been for many hundreds of years a lesson to us all?"

In an urgent voice Graham said, "Nothing can be accomplished without your people. Everyone knows how clever, and what good soldiers, the Druzes are. If I can tell them in Damascus that we have added the name of your tribe along with the tribe of Ismail to the Young Turks' cause, there will be much rejoicing, and when we are victorious, your people will be rewarded with greater independence."

"Ismail tells me you want us Druzes to make common cause with the Muslims, but Muhammad is not one of our prophets and the Koran is not our book. Our fight is as much against the Muslims as against the Turks and all unbelievers in the true religion. One day the Druzes will take Mecca."

Graham's hand reached up to caress the silky mane of the chieftain's horse, a large white stallion that was better groomed than his master. "Don't you see?" Graham said. "As long as the Arab people are at war with one another, nothing can be done to free them. Pray that there may be unity."

I could see from his expression that the chieftain did not like Graham touching his horse. He grew even more scornful. "We do not pray. *Our* god does not like us to meddle in his affairs."

"This Englishman will not come our way again," Ismail said to the chieftain. "Fate has brought him to us."

"Fate is for Islam," the chieftain said. "Our people are not crippled by fate. Our will is free, and we don't need the infidel to help us."

Graham said, "If you treasure freedom, you must see

that we are the ones to give it to you." With a twitch of its neck, the horse shook off Graham's hand.

"You are English. Why should you be interested in what happens in Turkey? In the past we have been friends with England, but now I think they want to spread their tents a little too far." The man wheeled his white stallion about and a moment later was gone.

Ismail shrugged. "I told you he would not be one of us," he said. There was no apology in his voice, only resignation. Before he rode away, he got off his horse and embraced Graham. "It takes only a few of us if we are strong," he said. A moment later he also was gone.

"You brought me here on purpose to meet those two men," I said.

"Yes," Graham said. "I don't apologize for wanting to make things better for these people. The trouble with you, Julia, is that you are content to be an onlooker."

"But I don't know enough to do anything."

Graham grasped me by the shoulders, and for a moment he looked so fierce, I was afraid he was going to shake me. Instead he said only, "Then trust me. Help me."

I chose sides: I chose Graham. Edith, my father, Monsieur Louvois, even Hakki—all were content for things to go on as they were so they could get what they wanted.

Only Graham wanted to change things. I knew he had done nothing for the poor woman in the sheikh's house, but surely he would find a way to help such women in the future. We walked back to the camp, my hand in Graham's. I tried to quiet the little voice inside of me that said, "First you let your father decide your life and now you are doing the same with Graham. When will you decide for yourself?"

We spent the rest of the afternoon getting ready for our departure. Edith, scattering sand and mud over the floor of the tent, was busy trying to force all the packaged bulbs and plants into her specimen bags; Monsieur Louvois was having a final exchange of money for precious objects with the Bedouin; and Graham was in his tent, writing.

In the early evening Father came looking for me. "Why don't we take a last trip to the ruins?" he suggested. "I don't suppose we'll see them again soon." The sun was low, so we were trailed by our long shadows. Father paused at one of the temples, a wave of dizziness overtaking him. He reached for my arm to steady himself.

I had been so taken up with the fate of the sheikh's niece that I had not noticed how tired my father looked; or if I had, I'd assumed it was a touch of dysentery, certainly something temporary. Now I realized he had not looked well for several days. "Something is wrong. You've lost weight," I said.

"I'm afraid I'm at the age when I should be an armchair traveler. A week or two of English rain and fog will have me well again."

I asked, "If your sheikh is friendly to Britain, do you believe the other Arabs will be friendly as well?"

Father said, "I would be more ready to believe it if Graham were not meddling. He is playing a dangerous game. The sultan hates the Young Turks, and he has his spies everywhere. Graham could end up in a Turkish prison, and believe me, there is not a more devilish place. I should be very sorry for him, but he will have no one to blame but himself."

Father's words were frightening. "But who would give Graham away?"

"People who live in the desert see everything. In all that emptiness they have nothing to study but their fellow man. Graham has been to a half dozen villages, spreading the Young Turks' revolution. But it is not Graham I care about. It is you. You might be implicated. I will not have my daughter going about with a man who would betray his country. What is even more dangerous is that he cares only about causes and not about people."

"But how would Graham's actions affect me?"

"It will be said that you and Graham are seen together.

Even if you are not arrested . . . if you have learned to care for Graham, what will you suffer when he is carried away bound and gagged on the back of a Turkish soldier's saddle?"

"I don't have the power to dissuade him."

"No, but you can stay away from him."

But whatever the danger, I didn't mean to stay away from Graham.

XIII

BEYOND FORKLUS

I COULD NOT WAIT to escape Palmyra and the hateful
sight of the sheikh's house with its hideous affair and
its counterfeit peacefulness. The rest of the party were
as ready to leave as I was. Monsieur Louvois's Bedouin were
staying away, their excavations for treasure exhausted. Edith,
having explored the flora around Palmyra, wanted to move
on, and Graham was anxious to reach Aleppo. Father
appeared tired, not only of Palmyra but weary of the whole
journey. Hakki only shrugged and said, "Nothing happens
unless it is predestined."

Our departure from Palmyra was ordered for daybreak;
Abdullah's idea was to cover as much distance as possible in
the cool of the morning. As the caravan departed, I noticed
the villagers begin to leave their houses and tents, ambling
in groups of twos and threes toward the temple. I asked
Hakki what was happening, but he wouldn't answer, irritated

with me for troubling him with a question whose answer I must guess. I did guess, and I wanted to leave Palmyra as quickly as I could. I urged a surprised Fadda to a canter and then on to something as close to a gallop as the horse, completely inexperienced in haste, could manage. When she resisted, I beat my heels against the horse's side, only to realize in my behavior how cruelty led to more cruelty. I feared that, as we had been so close to evil, a kind of curse had fallen on us and we would soon meet with some misfortune ourselves.

No one hurried after me, and soon I found myself alone in the desert with the others well behind me. My isolation was suddenly frightening. I reined in a relieved Fadda until Edith on her mount appeared on the horizon, first to join me, and then to calm me with an interminable tale of a race between herself and the late Professor Ladamacher to discover a variety of thornbush in the Hadhramaut. It didn't matter in the least to Edith that I was not listening: The tale was only a kindness on Edith's part.

For two days our caravan followed a shadow of low hills, blue in the morning when we set out and by afternoon a rich plum color. The spring rains had coaxed a prickle of green from the barren shingle and rock. Wherever a bit of soil clung to a rock, flowers bloomed in startling colors. Edith insisted over and over again on dismounting to examine them, and Hakki had to hurry her along.

Graham and I rode side by side. Occasionally Graham would lecture me, sometimes we would exchange tales of our childhood or tease each other; more often we were awed into silence by the vast empty spaces, exchanging looks rather than words. Father watched our growing familiarity with disapproval, but illness had so weakened him that he seemed to have lost the will to keep us apart.

On the third day the country changed. Beyond Forklus there was no green thing to be seen, only the sharpness of thorn and the hardness of rock. By late afternoon, and still miles short of Homs, Abdullah insisted, against Hakki's protests, that the horses were spent and we must stop and set up camp. He had picked a desolate place cradled by low, barren hills and with a doubtful well. In spite of Mastur's efforts to couch the camel beside the well and tempt it by forcing water into its mouth, the camel would have nothing to do with the well.

There was a small cluster of Bedouin tents in the distance, but an hour after our arrival, the tents and their occupants, men in robes and women in pointed straw hats and trousers with aproned skirts, were gone. If I had not had the sketches I had made of them to prove that they had been there, so quick and so complete was their disappearance, I would have doubted having seen them.

The mukaris fell easily into their old routine: Mohammed readied the tents; Mastur gave the camel its ration of barley, set a fire in the brazier, and began cutting up mutton for dinner; Habib brought a small container of water around, warning everyone, "There is only enough for the faces and hands. We must have water for coffee tonight and in the morning."

Edith and I were washing away some of the grime from the trip when Graham, with a brief apology, pushed his way through the flap of our tent. My heart always stopped when Graham appeared with no warning, for his image in real life was bolder and more reckless than the image I carried with me. His ginger hair was disheveled, his cheek streaked with soot, his shirt wrinkled and stained with sweat, and one boot was unlaced. Ignoring Edith, he sank down on one of the cots and drew me down beside him, putting his arm around me.

"I have rather worrying news, Julia. Your father tells me he has had some sort of spell. He's sitting up now, but he says he is nauseated and dizzy. I don't think it's his heart, but that's certainly a possibility. If we hadn't all been on the same diet, I would guess it was something he ate. At any rate, there is no way he can continue on horse-back tomorrow to Homs. What's needed is a carriage to take him. Mastur will ride on ahead of us to Homs to requisition a carriage. It should be here by tomorrow, noon, and it will take you and your father to Homs by late evening tomorrow—only a few hours after the rest of us have arrived by horseback."

I stared at Graham. "Tell me the truth. How ill is Father?"

"I'm sure it's nothing serious. As soon as we get to Homs, we'll make arrangements for him at the Jesuit hospital there. Hakki tells me they have very good doctors. I wanted to wait here with you and your father until the carriage comes, but for some reason your father is very firm in insisting that he doesn't want me—or Louvois or Edith either—to stay. Mohammed will remain behind with the two of you."

After a quick glance at Edith, Graham kissed my cheek lightly and left me to my misery. I accused myself of worrying about everything and everyone but the person closest to me. It had not occurred to me that Father's illness might be anything serious. I had no confidence in my ability to rise to an emergency and was terrified that something might happen to my father in the middle of nowhere with no one for him to depend on but myself and Mohammed, in whom I had little confidence. I had a premonition that it would be dangerous for Father and me to be left alone in the desert with no protection. I turned to Edith. "Why doesn't Hakki make everyone stay until the carriage comes?"

Edith patted my shoulder, rather like the comfort one gives a pitiful dog; you could almost hear a "good old boy" accompanying the reassurances. "We are short of water, for one thing," Edith said, "and for another, if I know your father, he insisted on us going on: He's not a man to want people about, coddling him and playing nursemaid. I'll leave you to get hold of yourself while I have a word with Mastur before he leaves for Homs. He can order some supplies for me. I am out of drying paper." On that businesslike note, Edith left.

Edith's lack of concern was irritating to me, but also reassuring. In the few moments it took me to reach my father's tent, I had pulled myself together. Father, resting in a camp chair, was prepared for me. Before I could get a word out, he said, "I hope you don't think my illness and my wanting to send the others on their way was some sort of ruse to keep you from Graham. I am sending Graham away because if he stayed, he and I would certainly get into some sort of argument, and I am not up to that."

Hurriedly I said, "Of course I don't think your illness is

any plot on your part. You haven't been looking well for days, and I should have done something about it."

Father smiled at this. "You're not to worry. Tomorrow we will ride to Homs quite comfortably in a carriage instead of having to jostle along on horseback with the others."

I could not help the selfish thought that if my father did have an illness, a heart condition or something of that sort, our trip would be at an end. I would not see Graham again. I had counted on another week with Graham, and now even that prospect was vanishing. I did not see how I could live in a world without him.

Father said, "Don't look so glum; I promise to recover. The trip isn't over—I still have things to accomplish."

In the morning, when it was time for the caravan to depart, everyone said how sorry they were to leave Father and me behind, but it was Hakki who was the most upset. "This is the last thing I wanted—that some of us should go forward and the others remain behind. This is a terrible thing, but what am I to do? We have little water and Mr. Hamilton orders us to leave. And this is not all I have to put up with. Miss Phillips has taken her horse and gone, leaving this note to tell me she is seeking some flower and will return shortly. That is too bad."

Edith's gear lay dispersed about the tent. I had been

asleep when she'd left, and I assumed now that she had not wanted to disturb me by shifting her boxes and cases about. Knowing it was nearly time for everyone to leave, I tried to gather her things together for her, reminding myself to tell her that I had discovered among some plant presses a package of drying paper that she must have overlooked. There had been no need to consult with Mastur about getting more. By the time I had all the gear packed, Edith was back, talking enthusiastically about a tulip she had found and leaving it for me to sketch. "It will make the time pass while you are waiting for the carriage," she said.

While the others were preparing to leave and Father was resting in his tent, Graham sought me out. "Julia, I want to stay with you, but I know it would upset your father and I have no wish to do that." He took my hand and put it inside his shirt so that I felt the damp warmth of his chest and the beat of his heart. "I'll keep you as close to me as that," he said, and left me.

Mohammed remained behind with ill grace. His face was sullen as he watched the others ride off. He even made a halfhearted attempt to follow them for a few yards until Graham sent him back with sharp words. I was as unhappy as Mohammed to see the others go. As I watched their figures disappear over the horizon, the desert seemed vaster than ever. For the second time on our journey I wished myself back in Durham Place, surrounded by houses and shops and streets full of people.

Mohammed squatted outside our tent, carrying on a conversation with his horse that was really meant for us, for the mumbling was in English. "They have left us behind in the desert, where we will remain until our flesh falls off our bones and even the vultures will not be able to make a decent meal of us." I thought that since the carriage was expected by noon and we would be in Homs by nightfall, there appeared to be something more to his worry than just our short delay, but I had no clue as to what it might be. I decided that with Father ill and Mohammed grumbling, I would have to be the one to assume responsibility. At first I was sure I would not be up to it, but as I thought about it, I decided it was a test. Had I finally traveled far enough in distance and in experience to watch over Father? I thought I had.

I ordered Mohammed to prepare morning tea. He went about it in a surly manner, grumbling that cooking was Mastur's work. He added water and salt to a mound of flour and viciously slapped the thick paste back and forth between his hands. When he had four flat discs, he threw them on the hot coals, managing to burn the two he gave to Father and me. Accompanying the scorched bread was a bit of goat cheese and a clump of sticky dates. After providing this feast, he took himself off to continue his sulking as though he could not bear our company another moment.

Father hardly touched his food. "I don't seem to have much of an appetite—not that this mess of Mohammed's would tempt a starving man. That fellow is good for nothing but helping Graham make trouble."

Eventually Mohammed fell asleep in the shade of the tent. Father and I were sitting at the tent's entrance, Father dozing in a camp chair and I cross-legged on a rug beside him, worrying over a sketch of the tulip Edith had left for me. Looking up, I noticed something on the horizon. At first I thought it was merely my nervous imagination, a mirage created by my worrying whether I would know what to do should Father become worse, for I was sure Mohammed would be no help. After a bit of watching, I began to believe in what I was seeing.

I woke my father. "There's something out there moving toward us. It can't be our carriage. It's coming from the direction of Palmyra."

We watched two figures on horseback materialize. Father said, "Those are the robes of the Metawileh tribe.

What can they want?" Suddenly he called, "Mohammed, come here quickly. *Yallah!*"

Mohammed, aroused by the alarm in Father's voice, appeared in the doorway of the tent. Father said, "Listen to me, Mohammed. We are going to have some visitors." Mohammed turned around quickly, and seeing the two riders, who were now clearly visible, he looked wildly about as if he meant to run away.

"If you are thinking of taking off, don't be a fool," Father said. "We know nothing about them. They may simply be passing through and perfectly harmless, but I want you to keep quiet. You are not to say a word. Give no indication that you understand or speak English. Now make a show of collecting our lunch things. *Yallah.*"

The two Metawilehs jumped from their horses and approached our camp at a rapid pace, their robes billowing out behind them. The face of the taller of the two was covered with a light bushy beard, so his round, red mouth had the appearance of a flower growing in a bed of straw. His eyes were blue and watchful. The other man lagged behind, his headdress pulled over much of his face. I hoped they could not hear the sound of Mohammed's heavy breathing, which seemed to fill the entire tent.

The first man said in quite good English, "We are sorry

to be a bother to you, but we have business we must attend to. We are looking for an Arab named Mohammed el Kahdi." He glanced in the direction of Mohammed.

"There is no one here by that name." Father said. "Apart from my daughter and me there is only our servant, Habib." Speaking in English to Mohammed, Father said, "Habib, get these men coffee." Mohammed was too frightened to move. "He understands almost no English," Father apologized, "and my Arabic is poor." Father, with nothing like his usual skill, repeated the command in a sort of pidgin Arabic, and after a pause Mohammed slunk quickly from the tent.

"We were a larger group," Father said, "and we had a mukari called Mohammed who was to stay with us, but at the last moment he went with the others, and Habib remained behind instead." The men studied Father. They hesitated, looking confused, as if they had been given the wrong information. I wondered where their information could have come from.

Mohammed appeared with the coffee, his hands trembling as he carried in the tray. Before the Metawilehs could notice Mohammed's shaking hands, and seeing that Father was too weak to make the effort, I got up and took the tray. "I will have the honor of serving our guests myself," I said, and handed around the small cups with as much courtesy as I could muster.

"This is a kindness on your part," the first man said. "The party we are after was seen riding into the villages near Palmyra with a henna-haired Englishman and filling the heads of the Druzes with some nonsense about supporting a new movement by the Young Turks. Why would such an Englishman come here to make trouble between the Muslims and the Druzes and plead the cause of the Turkish revolutionaries?"

"I am sorry for your trouble," Father said, "but I am pleased that this henna-haired Englishman you are looking for is in your country instead of his own, where he would undoubtedly be making trouble for me and my fellow countrymen."

The Metawilehs thought that was a good joke. "Yes, let the Englishman make uprisings here, where we know what to do with such men, but let him not make trouble between our tribes. That we cannot allow."

While he was talking, I was stealing glances at the second man, sure that I had seen him before. As he tipped his cup to get the last of the coffee, his kaffiyeh fell away from his face and I recognized the jagged scar I had seen on one of the Metawilehs who had returned Edith. I couldn't restrain a gasp. The man must have guessed what had happened, for he spoke a few urgent words to his companion. At that moment, from behind the tent came the clatter of a horse's hooves.

Startled, Father hurried outside, calling Mohammed's name. The two Metawilehs ran for their horses.

As they took off, the taller of the two said to Father, "Now you call him 'Mohammed'!"

Father sank down on the chair. His face was gray and pinched with worry and beaded with drops of sweat. He took out his pocket handkerchief, which was ridiculously clean and unwrinkled, as if it could not possibly have made our difficult journey.

As he watched the two men take off, Father said to me, "Calling out Mohammed's name was very stupid of me. I like to think that if I were well, I would not have been so careless. There is nothing more to be done. I believe there was a chance we might have saved Mohammed if he had trusted us." When Father saw my dismay, he added, "You are not to worry. Those men were after Mohammed. They mean no harm to us. I must tell you, Julia, that I was impressed with your composure."

I was pleased by Father's words, but I was furious with Graham. Because of his obsession with his secret society of Young Turks, Mohammed's life was in jeopardy. "Graham got Mohammed into this trouble," I said.

I expected my father to agree, but he was more philo-sophical. "Graham's enthusiasm makes him thoughtless. He wishes to save the world and thinks in terms of hundreds of thousands of people. I'm afraid Mohammed's life is no more to him than a means to an end."

I was about to tell my father that I had recognized one of the Metawileh, when he said, "The excitement has rather tired me. I'm going to have a little nap. By the time I awake, the carriage should be here."

Not wanting to upset him, I decided to say nothing of my suspicions. It was high noon, and there were no shadows to give depth to the empty scene, only the rocky plain like a sheet of shimmering silver in the sun. High above, in the foothills, I saw a quick movement. For a moment I thought it might be Mohammed's white robe, but it was a gazelle leaping playfully about the rocks. It leaped higher and higher until I could not be sure whether I saw the animal or only my memory of it. Dazzled by the heat and light, I found a bit of shade under a tree and fell asleep. When I awoke, it was late afternoon, long past the time for the carriage's arrival. Father was awake as well.

"What will we do if the carriage doesn't come?" I asked. "It might be days before someone passes this way. We have very little water and almost no food, and Mohammed took the only horse. Even if I started out on foot to find help, I wouldn't know in what direction to turn." I thought it was very far for us to come just to die.

"You are certainly not to consider walking off into the desert; that is your romanticism at its most bizarre. If we have not arrived in Homs by tonight, Hakki will send someone to find us. We are not the kind of people who are misplaced."

Just before dark I discovered a cache of food Mohammed had squirreled away for his own pleasure. It was not much: dates and dried apricots, a little rice and coffee as well. I gathered a bundle of thorn branches as I had seen Mastur do and started a fire so we could boil the rice. With the darkness the desert cooled quickly, and we kept the fire burning long after dinner. The very largeness of the desert gave a snug feeling to our den. I had worried that I might not manage, but here I was with Father at night in the middle of the desert, and I had.

As the fire died away and darkness fell, I said, "I wish you would turn in, Father. You look so ill." When he hesitated, I promised, "I'll join you—I'm tired as well." Yet neither one of us made a move to go inside the tent; it was enough that we sat near its shelter.

I had never felt closer to my father, but our very closeness kept me from talking of what I most longed to—Graham, and how I was trying to reconcile how much I cared for him with my anger at his involving Mohammed in his schemes. I didn't want to spoil what my father and I had and might not have again—comradeship, something completely new in our relationship.

"You really must not be concerned about me," Father said. "I want you to know, Julia, that this has been a journey for me, not only to far lands but in how I have come to see you for the fine, intelligent young woman you are. I am afraid that after your mother died, I tried to lose myself in my work, neglecting what should have been most precious to me. I hope it is not too late to make amends."

I took his hand, unable to find words.

The fire died out and we moved into the tent. Father insisted I have the cot while he slept in the camp chair. I awoke two or three times during the night, each time with something close to panic; I listened for the sound of my father's breathing, giving thanks when I heard it. At dawn we were awakened by the soft calls of the rock doves.

In the late morning a carriage appeared on the horizon. In minutes Edith was climbing out and coming toward us, her walk firm and purposeful, someone sure of her ground.

"Well, you're very cozy here," she said, smiling. There

was envy in her voice, as though nothing could be nicer than to be abandoned by everyone and left alone in the middle of the desert. There was also a firmness to her step, as if she had a task to accomplish, but I put that down to her wish to rescue us.

"This is very good of you, Edith," Father said. "I have to admit I'm not sorry to see a familiar face."

"Even mine? The truth is we were all worried. Graham wanted to come with the carriage, but I thought he had done enough mischief out here. I meant to come myself, and quite clever I was, too, telling Graham the carriage was to leave an hour later than I ordered it for. He'll be quite furious."

"Edith," I asked, "why didn't they send the carriage yesterday as they were supposed to?"

"When we got to Homs, Hakki was busy with tucking everyone into their rooms at the hotel and making arrangements for our trip to Aleppo. He believed Mastur when Mastur told him a carriage was on its way to you, but when he finally got around to checking with the company, he found Mastur had never ordered the carriage.

"At any rate," Edith went on, "Mastur has taken off, and good riddance. I don't know how I could have been so foolish as to trust that man. Hakki was in a terrible state, worrying that you were alone all night with no one besides Mohammed to keep the jinn away. By the way, where is Mohammed?"

I told the story.

"I can't say I was sorry to see Mohammed take off," Father said. "He was more of a liability than a help. Still, if they catch the fellow, it won't go well with him."

"I'm afraid Graham has to take the responsibility for that," Edith said. "He had no business involving Mohammed in his schemes—whatever they were."

I was troubled by Mastur's trickery. I didn't believe it was a thing he would have done on his own. He must have received orders from someone to leave us alone in the desert. The delay in the carriage was clearly a means of giving the Metawilehs a chance to get at Mohammed. That could mean trouble eventually for Graham, but it had also put Father and me in grave danger. It frightened me to think there must be someone in our group who wished us harm.

Before I could share my worries with Edith, she said, "I think we ought to be on our way at once. Awad, who is our driver, is perfectly competent. He'll have us in Homs by evening."

Our bags, long since packed, were quickly stowed, so in no time we were headed for Homs. As the carriage pulled away, I scanned the hills. "Mohammed might have escaped and perhaps is up there."

"Don't trouble yourself," Edith said. "Even if the man escaped his captors, he will be too ashamed of his desertion to show his face."

When the horses were running well, the breeze made the inside of the carriage tolerable; when the road was poor and the horses had to pick their way over rough stones, slowing the carriage, it was stifling. At noon we stopped for lunch at a small village where Edith insisted we stay long enough for Father to rest, even finding some broth for him when the rough food didn't tempt him. But the rest and the broth did nothing to make him better; in fact, he became so weak, I worried that we might not reach Homs in time. I urged Edith to make Awad start out at once, but she insisted that Father needed a bit of rest.

"A nap will be much better for him than jostling along in a carriage."

While we rested, Awad, after seeing to the horses, wandered into the village to learn the local news. He returned to the camp with a story of a pair of Metawilehs coming through the town with a man riding pillion. The man had been trussed. "Who is this unfortunate man?" Awad had asked, and was told, "We do not know the customs of the place where you have come from, but in our village a man's business is his own."

"Surely," Awad said, "the unfortunate man was Mohammed."

Father slept in the carriage's shadow, while Edith and I wandered a short distance up the *jebel*, or hill, to find our own patch of shadow under a thorn bush. "I haven't had a chance to tell my father," I said, "but I recognized one of the men who came for Mohammed." I described the scar on the man's throat. "I know it was one of the Metawilehs who tried to collect the money in Jerud for your return."

"Are you suggesting that they are following us?"

"What else can I think?"

"I'm not sure I would worry your father with that little fantasy. A knife scar is common enough in this country. At any rate, it appears they have Mohammed by now, poor devil. I don't suppose we shall see them again."

"This trip is so different from what I had imagined, Edith. I thought travel of this kind was carefree, that one was just shown things. I hadn't planned to worry or think. At most, I saw myself doing a little sketching and having friendly conversations with fellow travelers. It never occurred to me that the people I traveled with would have anything on their minds other than amusement. Yet every day, almost every hour, there has been some sort of crisis, and now Father's illness is the greatest worry of all. I have to believe someone wishes us harm. I don't know whom I can trust. You and Monsieur Louvois are the only ones who seem not to want to stir up trouble."

"I am not sure Louvois is so innocent," Edith said. "He may be an enthusiastic collector, but he is also a well-connected Frenchman, and France has long had a lustful eye on Syria. Why should we believe he might not drop a hint here and there? If the French get their greedy hands on Syria, they will destroy it. They have no use for indigenous cultures—they recognize no culture but their own."

I was growing more apprehensive by the minute. "Edith," I pleaded, "hadn't we better be on our way? At this rate we'll never make Homs by dark."

In the afternoon heat the horses were listless, forcing Awad to urge them on with coaxing and finally curses. Father was weaker, and twice we had to stop so that he could get rid of the little broth he had managed to get down. Edith tried to get him to drink some water, which she flavored with a bit of lemon and sugar she had thoughtfully brought with her, but he shook his head. At last the sun lowered, and the twilight coolness crept down from the surrounding hills to relieve the desert heat. Ahead of us were the lights of the town of Homs. As we drew near, I was startled to see in the growing darkness the city all but disappear.

Puzzled, I said, "There are lights, but they seem to hang in a black sky."

Edith explained, "The houses in Homs are built of black basalt. It's the native stone."

I shuddered at entering a city the color of mourning.

XIV

H O M S

ATHER GRUMBLED ABOUT having to go to the hospital. "There is nothing wrong with me that a rest in a hotel with a proper bed and some decent food won't cure."

Edith strongly agreed. "A hospital cannot be a good place for a sick person. I would be more than pleased to take care of you. I've learned something of nursing from years on my own in the desert."

In spite of Edith's kind offer of help, I would not be swayed. In the desert, knowing that my father depended on me for the first time in my life, I had felt my own strength and experienced the heady taste of authority. Over Edith's and Father's objections I directed Awad to have the carriage take us to the Jesuit hospital. I was all the more sure that my father must be ill when, after some halfhearted protests, he gave in.

After the heat and dust of the desert, the cool corridors

and immaculate white rooms of the hospital were another world. "Good Lord," Father murmured. "Clearly nuns have been at work." He agreed to one night "in clean sheets." As soon as he was settled in, he ordered Edith and me to go. "There's nothing for you to do here," he told us, "and you'll want a chance to clean up and get a decent meal."

A sister appeared to take possession of her patient, letting us know she was eager to be rid of us. "We must give our patient a good scrubbing. Then we will call in the doctors." Father gave a weak smile at her priorities.

Waiting for us at the entry of the hotel was an abject Hakki. He was effusive in his apologies for the delay of the carriage. "How can I ever make amends? If Watson and Sons learned of this, it would be the end of everything for me. I knew if we did not all stay together, something very bad would come about.

"How could Mohammed have deserted you?" he went on. "And what a terrible thing is his punishment. What can Mastur have been thinking, to run away without ordering the carriage? Why must I have fools around me? May Allah reward them according to their deeds. If I had not checked on the carriage myself, you and your father might still be there in the desert."

At that I shivered, for I doubted that Father would have

survived another day in the heat.

The Grand Hotel was not a hotel at all but a kind of boardinghouse. The lobby was a small sitting room crowded with soiled, overstuffed furniture and lamps with shades of rotted silk that dripped fringe. The proprietor, rubbing his hands, hurried out from behind the desk to greet us. He was smiling widely, showing off very white false teeth. His fez with its tatty tassel was not unlike the lampshades. The man had many questions and suggestions as to what he might do for us, but Hakki, after ordering a light dinner to be brought up to me, took me off to my room and, with further apologies, urged me to get a good night's rest.

"If your father is well enough, the day after tomorrow we will all leave for Aleppo, but only if he is well enough. Never again will one person be here and another there."

With great pride he said, "We take the railroad, which is only two years old and very modern, so it will be more convenient than the horses and tents and more restful for your father. You will sit in comfortable seats and compartments. I have myself, once, sat in these seats and they are like a mother's lap. You will have nothing to do but look out from your window and rest." Hakki closed the door softly behind him as though I were already asleep.

Alone for the first time in days, I gave myself over to

worrying about my father. I was sure someone had instructed Mastur not to order the carriage. Had Father taken a turn for the worse, the delay might have meant the difference between life and death. I was also sure I had recognized the Metawileh who had returned Edith. I wondered if he had been following us all along, and if he had, why?

I lay down on the bed, longing for sleep to put an end to all the questions. Sleep came to the sound of the muezzin's call to evening prayer. *Allahu akbar. Ash'hadu an la ilaha illa-llah:* "God is great. I bear witness that there is no God but God." Those were Muslim words, but the God was the God of everyone. I gave thanks that He had been watching over us.

When I awoke, night had darkened my window. From somewhere I heard a quiet but insistent knocking—not a servant's knock—and realized it was what had awakened me. I thought it might be Hakki again and, half asleep, opened the door to find Graham, looking sheepish. He was wearing not his camping khakis but the suit he had worn when we'd first met on the steamer from Istanbul to Beirut. The suit was freshly cleaned and pressed, and in the small shabby room Graham looked very handsome, like a king who shows himself in all his glory to cheer his beggared subjects.

He sank down onto a chair. "Hakki told me what

happened and gave me a scolding for having involved Mohammed, poor fellow, in my project. It must have been horribly frightening."

"It was upsetting for Father, but it was more frightening for Mohammed. You encouraged him to take dangerous risks, and then you left him. He could be dead. He probably is."

"You have every reason to be angry with me, but I had no way of knowing your father would be taken ill and it would be Mohammed who would be left behind. I had thought if there was trouble, I would be there to explain that Mohammed had nothing to do with my interests and was merely under my hire. In any event, my cause is greater than one man."

"You want to save the world, but you couldn't keep one man out of harm's way. You couldn't even save that poor woman's life."

"I have a great reluctance to tamper with the religious practices of others. There has been enough of that." Graham gave me a tight smile. "I've been rude, lecturing you after the shocking time you've had. However indifferent you may believe me to be, I am upset about Mohammed. However, I can't forget that it was Hakki who asked that Mohammed stay behind; it was also your father who made the occasion with his 'illness.' I will be interested in seeing what the doctors find, if indeed they find anything."

"You can't be seriously accusing my father of making up his illness to put Mohammed in danger?"

"No, of course not. Now I must let you get back to sleep. I apologize for awakening you, but surely you weren't sleeping in your clothes?"

"I was too tired to change."

He knelt down beside the edge of the bed where I was sitting and gently removed my shoes. Then he picked me up and settled me in the bed, covering me with the sheet and bending over to kiss me. At the door he asked, "Do you forgive me?"

For an answer I only smiled.

At breakfast Hakki announced, "When we reach Aleppo, we will have a new dragoman and other mukaris. Miss Phillips recommended to me a dragoman with whom she has traveled in the past."

"You won't have trouble with Khidr," Edith said. "Of course you will still want to keep an eye on him. I am only sorry we are making the trip from Homs to Aleppo by rail. There is so much one misses; it maddens me to catch a glimpse of a tempting plant through a train window."

"I for one find the idea of traveling by railroad *délicieuse*,"

Monsieur Louvois said. "Never will I get all the sand and dust from my clothes. And the sooner we get to northern Syria, the better. I have heard there are some quite pretty things being offered in Antioch. Five thousand years ago there was a great city there."

Graham gave him a dark look. "Why are you so interested in what happened five thousand years ago and so little interested in what is happening to this country now? It seems a selfish attitude."

"*Au contraire.* There is much to be learned from what happened five thousand years ago, and the lesson is plain: This, too, shall pass away. With that lesson always before me, why should I concern myself with what is happening now? The civilization we have around us here is not producing anything of great beauty; and it is beauty that I am looking for. At least I can say I am not leaving this country any the worse for my visit, which is more than some of us can say." He gave Graham a stern look.

Hakki hastily interrupted. "Our trip is nearly over. Surely, gentlemen, you can be civil to each other for so short a time. We will leave for the station first thing tomorrow morning. Miss Hamilton, the doctor of your father encourages me to believe your father will be well enough to travel with us."

On the way to the hospital, with my memory of Graham's kiss and with Hakki's assurance that my father was better, I was almost cheerful. With a thought of amusing my father, I was rehearsing a description of how Edith had found a rare plant on the hotel grounds, which the proprietor of the hotel would not allow her to carry off. At midnight the proprietor had discovered her in his garden with a trowel. He wanted to throw her out of the hotel, and Hakki had to be awakened to soothe the man, who had then posted a guard next to the plant.

When I got to my father's room, I found it empty, the bed stripped of its sheets, the mattress rolled up, the shutters closed. My first reaction to the deserted room was one of panic. Hospital rooms that suddenly became empty meant death.

Then I heard, "Oh, mademoiselle, your father left a half hour ago." The sister who hurried in was shy, with enormous eyes and a charming French accent. No, she had no idea where he might have gone; but with delicate hands she drew out of her apron pocket an envelope. I read my name in my father's familiar handwriting, which always looked to me hurried—as though it were written not in haste, but with impatience. "Julia, I am much improved and am tending to a little business. I will return to the hotel this afternoon and will see you there."

I thanked the sister, and was about to hurry away, when a look of concern on her face stopped me. "Is my father really all right?" I asked.

"He is fine now, mademoiselle; however, there is a worry I am afraid he does not take seriously."

"Is it his heart?"

"He is in good health, mademoiselle, but I believe someone wishes otherwise, for your father was poisoned."

"Poisoned!" I sank down onto the one chair in the room. "Are you sure?"

"Oh, there is no doubt. We have the finest toxicologist in the country working for us. I didn't mean to alarm you; I only wanted to protect your father, who seems a fine gentleman." Before I could ask more questions, she had vanished into the hospital corridors.

I hurried at once to the hotel, anxious to see Father but hoping to avoid seeing anyone else, for the moment they saw me, they would know something was wrong, and yet I felt I shouldn't tell them the sister's story until I had talked with my father. It was late afternoon when Father knocked on my door, pale but obviously determined to convince me he was well. It was the first time I had ever seen a need on his part to impress me. "I am perfectly fine," he said, but I saw how gratefully he settled down onto a chair. "Two days' rest on the train will have me right again."

"Father, tell me the truth. I've talked with the sister and she said you were poisoned."

"Ah, well, I hadn't meant you to hear that. The doctors at the hospital were first-rate but a bit dramatic. They seem to think I have been ingesting a poisonous plant: *Conium maculatum*; in layman's language some form of Syrian hemlock. But that is all nonsense."

"That someone wanted to poison you can't be dismissed as nonsense."

"I have told you, Julia, that I don't believe the doctors, and I caution you about discussing their bizarre diagnosis with our fellow travelers. That must be a secret between us. There is something much more serious to discuss. I have been thinking over this thing with Graham."

While I was trying to absorb his calm reaction to the startling fact that he might have been poisoned, Father went on. "I think it is time, Julia, that you understood exactly why Graham is taking this trip. When you do, I am sure you will realize that you cannot do anything to support Graham's position; that, in fact, what Graham is doing is seriously jeopardizing not only my mission but the interests of my country and, I might point out, your country as well."

I was frightened by the seriousness of Father's tone and felt my small authority over him dissolve. I wanted to say Graham had already confided in me, that I knew what he was about; but some caution or suspicion made me wait to hear what Father had to say.

"In Graham's attempts to stir up support for the Young Turks, he has been making contact with a secret society here in Syria. This society is ruled by a man named Abdul Aziz al Masri. Were this band interested only in Arab independence from the Ottoman Empire, that would be one thing, but al Masri wishes to spread this desire for independence to our colony of India. Just lately the British Foreign Office has had intelligence that there have been uprisings in India, and even acts of anarchy and sedition against the British government, which can be traced to the interference of the Young Turks. British lives have been endangered in India as a result of al Masri's interference, to say nothing of his trying to overturn British rule there. You see how foolhardy it would be to become involved with that kind of thing."

"But what is wrong with the Arab people wanting their independence from the Ottoman Empire, or the Indian people, for that matter, wanting their independence from England?"

"What you don't understand is that we are not speaking of one Arab people or one Indian people. There are numerous sects of Muslims, many of whom do not get along. They kill one another over the possession of a well; what would they do over the possession of a country? It may be that one day something could be done to give them a measure of independence—under British oversight, of course—but that is for the future. Just now England has the French breathing down its neck, wanting Syria for their own. As for India, if the British got out, the Hindus and Muslims would be at one another with knives." There was no conviction in Father's voice. He seemed to be explaining out of habit, as if his heart were no longer in his words.

"There is no need to bore you with this, Julia. I am telling you only to let you see where your friendship with Geddes might lead." He gave me a close look. "And I trust it is no more than a casual friendship. Of course, you understand that I tell you this in the strictest confidence."

"But Father," I protested. "You didn't suggest when we left London that I was under some obligation to uphold the imperial interests of the British Empire—nor am I sure I want to."

I was proud of my speech but afraid my father would be outraged. Instead he was annoyed, which made my speech sound ridiculous. "I have been proud of you, Julia. You have managed very well on this trip, and I have seen with pleasure how you have changed from a young girl with limited interests into a young woman who takes an interest in everything; but I must warn you against doing anything that would hinder my purposes here, or it will be Geddes who must answer for the consequences."

In the morning, seeing that Father was well enough to travel and knowing nothing of what the doctors suspected, Hakki took our little group to the train, where he shepherded us into our compartments. The compartments, though far from luxurious, were as Hakki had promised, new and comfortable. The men shared two sleeping rooms and Edith and I another.

My last image of Homs was a row of basalt minarets piercing the blue sky like black arrows. The train followed the valley of the Orontes River into the city of Hama; there the train stopped long enough for Edith to hand some money through the window for a paper of dates, which we ate hungrily with sticky fingers. Just outside Hama there were enormous waterwheels large as a Ferris wheel, emptying the river out onto the parched fields. From time to time the train crossed the wayward river, so first it would be on one side of us and then on the other, but the Nosairiyeh Mountains stayed always on our right like a bookmark.

On the dusty plains, little villages appeared with beehive-roofed houses and always with a child or two standing in silent and forlorn attention as our train passed. For me the days on the train were welcome. Light breezes came through the windows, and at night the swaying train rocked me to sleep. While on the train I felt enclosed in a kind of protective armor that allowed me to see everything but kept anything evil from touching me or Father. I was almost sorry when we drew into Aleppo.

Aleppo was too large, the inhabitants rude and sullen, the city dusty, and the streets full of the litter of centuries. We gathered in the hotel's parlor, where we were served tea in diminutive Turkish coffee cups requiring constant refilling.

"I saw Louvois getting into a carriage," Edith said. "He gave the address of Monsieur Arnould, who happens to be the French consul."

Graham looked interested. "I should have thought with his rather shady trading, he would want to stay well away from the authorities."

"I've had some rather surprising information," Father said. "It appears that Louvois . . ." But before he could finish,

Hakki bore down upon us, a look of bewildered hurt on his face. The proper dark suit and slicked-back hair, the injured dignity and pouting mouth, all gave him the look of a child who has carefully dressed for a party to which he has been forbidden to go.

"One of you has been most unkind. I have had a letter from Watson and Sons telling me that there have been complaints about my service."

"We're sorry to hear it," Graham said, "but why blame one of us?"

"Watson and Sons tell me in their letter that someone on this tour has written to complain of me. I have done all I could do. The bad things that happened were not my fault. Please tell me how I have offended."

"There must be some misunderstanding," Edith said. "I shall write to Watson and Sons myself, and at once. You have done your job very well, and I've said so from the start."

Half to himself Hakki said, "If they hear of these complaints, the government will be unhappy."

Father asked sharply, "I thought you were a schoolmaster. What have you to do with the Turkish government?"

Hakki looked flustered. "What do you suggest? Do you accuse me of spying? I deny it absolutely."

"Nonsense," Edith said. "We accuse you of nothing of the kind, and I will see that it all comes right." Hakki left, only partly mollified.

Graham said, "After all, Hakki taught in a military school, so I wouldn't be in the least surprised to find he has been working for the Turks as well as Watson and Sons. We know the Turks keep an eye on any group that travels through Syria, certainly one in which they suspect their visitors of an official connection." Graham looked accusingly at Father.

Later, as Father and I were on our way to our rooms to dress for dinner, I asked, "What were you going to tell us about Louvois?"

"I was going to say that Louvois has a connection or two with the French government—not official, of course, but nonetheless interesting. I suppose he is acting as their eyes and ears. One of the reasons I am here is to keep France out of Syria."

"How did you find out about Louvois?"

"When I got out of the hospital at Homs, I wired the Foreign Office to check on him; one doesn't have to be in diplomacy for very long before one senses when a Frenchman has an eye out for a little real estate."

"Did you ask the Foreign Office about anyone else on

our tour?" I was sure he had made inquiries about Graham.

"There is nothing wrong in wanting to know about one's playmates, particularly when one is supposed to have been poisoned."

XV

AIN EL BEIDA

WE LEFT ALEPPO WITH the new dragoman who had been procured by Edith; and with the dragoman came two mukaris, Daud and Mustafa. Daud was young, no more than eighteen or nineteen, eager and chatty, with melting brown eyes. Mustafa was older and more reserved, brisk and busy, a man who looked as though he did not like to be ordered about. The dragoman, Khidr, was thin and hollow cheeked and would not look at you. His hair hung in untidy ringlets, and a wisp of chin whisker decorated a sullen face. He missed very little. When Monsieur Louvois refused to trust his small leather case to the mukaris and insisted instead on handling it himself, Khidr's eyes followed the case as Louvois secured it in his saddlebag.

In Ain el Beida we were to stay in a sheikh's house rather than in tents, so the caravan was traveling lightly. We started off on a road of stone blocks. "They were laid by the

Romans two thousand years ago," Hakki informed us. There was no enthusiasm in his voice, only duty; he could not get over his betrayal to Watson & Sons.

The Romans had tired quickly, or perhaps they had run out of slaves, for their road dwindled to nothing, leaving us to cross a dry plain where the sun punished us and a cloud of reddish dust settled angrily on our clothes and horses. When I wiped the sweat from my face, the dust left red smears. In no time we looked like a troupe of clowns. The horse that had taken Fadda's place resisted the rough ground, and my back ached from the awkward ride. After an hour or two the land grew greener. There were olive and almond orchards. Fields of barley shivered in the wind, and tangles of blackberry brambles grew along the wayside. I could almost imagine myself on a country road in England.

In the middle of the day we stopped for lunch and a rest in the small village of Tokat. I settled myself next to Graham, with the others close by, all of us grateful for the pool of shade provided by an orchard of fig trees. The animals and gear were given over to the mukaris to care for, but Khidr insisted on seeing to them himself, sending Daud and Mustafa to prepare lunch. "The horses are overly tired with the heat, *effendi*," Khidr said to Hakki. "I will take care of them so they are rested and fresh for the afternoon." Unlike me, Hakki did not see the expression of helpfulness on the dragoman's face turn to hate the moment Hakki turned his back.

The mukaris poured water into basins for us so that we could wash away the red dust, then gave us a lunch of cheese and flatbread followed by dates and oranges and hot tea, which was refreshing now that we had cooled off. The setting for our meal could not have been prettier. Butterflies progressed in an orderly fashion among a sprinkling of wild crocuses that Edith was already sampling. After our lunch we lay under the trees and chatted in a lazy way, except for Edith, who covered her face with her straw hat and went immediately to sleep, her soft wheezing snores as soothing as the sound of a gentle surf. If it hadn't been for the mukaris hunched nearby, we might have been picnicking in the English countryside.

When we returned to the horses, Khidr, full of un-convincing smiles, greeted us with a new sprightliness that, for no reason I knew, alarmed me.

We descended into the wadi and had an easy ride of only a few hours to Ain el Beida. Graham explained to me that in many small villages, where no stopping places existed for travelers, it was usual for a party to stay in the home of the local sheikh. The custom had existed for thousands of years:

In a world of desert and empty distances, hospitality is a matter of life and death.

We were welcomed by Sheikh Abd el Rehman, a tall, upright man with a tangled beard, kindly eyes, fat cheeks, and a rifle slung so comfortably over his shoulder that he might have been born with it. The sheikh greeted us gracefully and, after assigning a servant, a young black man, to care for our horses, ushered us into a small house made with the sun-dried brick of the countryside. The sheikh left us for a moment to see to some detail of our accommodations and Monsieur Louvois said to no one in particular, "That black man is a slave. *Quel disgrâce.*"

"To give them their due, the Turks have outlawed slavery in most of the Ottoman Empire," Father said. "They were bullied into allowing the Arabs to keep on with it." He turned to Graham. "What will your idealistic Young Turks do about that?" he asked.

Graham said, "Don't preach to me. My father fought against the Boers at Ladysmith and Mafeking. He said the British were fighting the war for all the Africans. When the peace was made, England went back on its promise of a vote for the native Africans."

"We have forbidden slavery in South Africa," Father countered.

Graham said, "Without the black man's right to vote, slavery is merely a technical term."

We were shown to our quarters by one of the sheikh's servants. The room to which Edith and I were assigned was small but freshly whitewashed, with a shuttered window that looked out onto a courtyard where the veiled women of the household went back and forth like black shadows. I liked this intimacy with another kind of life and wondered if we would have the opportunity of visiting the harem to meet the women of the house; and then, remembering my last visit to a harem, I shuddered.

In the late afternoon Edith pulled on her boots and shouldered her knapsack to go off in search of plants, while Father and Graham, each reluctant to leave the other alone with the sheikh, stayed behind. Monsieur Louvois and I walked the short distance into the village with Hakki, who promised us ancient tombs. Once in the village, Paul Louvois thought of an unconvincing errand he had to attend to, leaving Hakki and me to go on alone to the tombs, which were hardly more than crevices among the rocks with a few carvings and an unroofed stone stairway open to the heavens.

Hakki was in a quiet and joyless mood. He spoke not so much to me as to some gods who had disappointed him.

"Nothing good will come from this trip," he said. "It was to be a pleasant journey, and I was to show all the things to be seen. I looked into many books in preparation for the trip. I went to much trouble in the arrangements. But it is not knowledge and pleasure that everyone desires, but an opportunity to make trouble for my country and for me."

I tried to cheer him. "I've enjoyed myself immensely, Hakki, and so have the others. We'll all write to Watson and Sons to tell them so. And it isn't your country the others are criticizing, only the sultan."

Hakki drew himself up. "Miss Hamilton, the sultan *is* the country." After that we walked among the dull tombs, slapping at flies and keeping silent.

In the evening the sheikh, his tangled beard wagging amiably as he spoke, extended a gracious invitation for us to dine with him. We ate in the Arab fashion, sitting in a companionable circle on rather shabby and stained rugs, reaching with our right hands into a large communal brass dish of mutton and rice. We were joined by members of the sheikh's family—brothers, cousins, in-laws; all men of course—who had no English or no wish to speak it, but sat silently staring at us, giving the impression that here indeed was something novel. After a few awkward confrontations I learned there was a nice etiquette as to when one's turn came, so that a bowl full of greedy hands was avoided.

The sheikh was full of questions as to where we were going and where we had been. He dismissed Aleppo and Antioch. "Cities do not interest me," he said. "In the city the small courtesies are the first thing lost. The next thing is your money. And the thing after that is your freedom. I remain in my own village, where I can read in each man's face a familiar story."

Edith, in a flirtatious mood we had not seen before, set out to woo the sheikh, praising everything in sight—rugs, servants, food—and lapsing frequently into Arabic. I was startled by her coquetry and would not have been surprised had she reached over and pinched the man's fat cheeks or chucked him under his double chin. For his part the sheikh appeared entranced by the stout, middle-aged woman with the mannish haircut and rumpled, baggy clothes, treating her as though she were some perfumed, dark-eyed dancing girl wrapped in silk scarfs and veiled in gauze. He picked out the best nuggets of mutton for her and filled her coffee cup himself. His relatives, observing his behavior out of the corners of their eyes, appeared to regard it as an amusing game.

"She's as good as bewitched him," Graham muttered to me. "I wouldn't be surprised to see her moving into his harem."

After dinner the relatives viewed the empty bowls with regret and withdrew. The sheikh invited Edith to examine a rose of unusual color in his courtyard, and Hakki went off in search of Khidr, who seemed to have disappeared.

Monsieur Louvois said, "While he's gone, I must show the three of you a most *élégant* find. It was brought to me by a man I contacted this afternoon in the village. He said they discover these things just south of here, and more things are available. It is possible I may stay another day at the sheikh's house and rejoin you in Antioch." As Monsieur Louvois spoke, he was unwrapping a small stone statue, which he then thrust at us with the air of a magician exceeding his usual tricks. "Have you ever seen anything with more majesty? It is four, perhaps five thousand years old."

The statue, about seven inches high, was of a man, haughty and magisterial, a king or priest whose almond-shaped eyes stared straight out with the expression of a sovereign weighed down with boredom. His chest was bare, but he wore a skirt made of carved petallike tiers. The long beard was curled into an intricate pattern suggesting unlimited vanity.

The three of us were dumb with admiration. Finally Graham said, "It's very fine, but you've no right to take it away from this place. It belongs here."

"*Absurde.* It will be sold to the next person who comes along."

"Apart from the ethics of the thing," Father said, "you can get into a great deal of trouble, and so could we for being associated with you."

Graham agreed. "I second Hamilton. You are putting all of us at risk."

Monsieur Louvois's look went from stubborn to nasty. "You are hardly the one to speak of getting us in trouble, Geddes. I talked with Abdullah in Homs and found out what happened to Mohammed."

"What I do, I do for a principle; what you do, you do for greed," Graham snapped.

"You are very clever if you believe you can separate the one from the other," Louvois told him.

I was growing to dread these squabbles among the three men, for the anger never seemed to be about the thing they were arguing over, but about some hidden disagreement that was never resolved because it was never spoken of.

Edith, flushed and grinning, returned from her tête-à-tête with the sheikh and scolded, "You are as quarrelsome as schoolboys. You never tire of your scraps. Perhaps we will have something less theoretical to deal with, for there is Hakki returning without Khidr."

Hakki, usually so neat even in the middle of the desert, appeared with his hair rumpled and his jacket unbuttoned. He had the panicky look of a man who realizes he has lost control. "This is unfortunate," he said. "Our dragoman, Khidr, is nowhere to be found. If he doesn't return by the morning, we will have to trust ourselves to the mukaris. I don't like it, but what else can we do?"

Later, as we were getting ready for bed, Edith said to me, "Nothing seems to be going well: the plot against Mohammed, Hakki's fall from grace, your father's illness, and now Khidr sneaking away—not at all like him." With a sigh she reached for the Koran.

"Graham once told me unbelievers were forbidden to touch the Koran."

"'Let none touch it but the purified'; but I am of the opinion that if one lives long enough in the desert, one is indeed purified."

In the morning the mukaris sulked and drew circles in the dust with their sandals. "No, *effendi*," Daud told Hakki, "we cannot leave without Khidr. He is sure to return soon."

Mustafa supported Daud. "Khidr told us under no condition were we to leave without him."

Hakki became even more indignant, seeing the delay as one more mark against him with Watson & Sons. "Why should he have given you those instructions and said nothing to me about his leaving or returning? We are already an hour late in our start." He appealed to the sheikh. "We must reach Antioch tomorrow."

Sheikh Abd el Rehman was looking out over the plain. "I would gladly send one of my men with you, but I believe your Khidr returns." There was a note of warning in his voice.

By now we could make out on the horizon three figures riding toward us. The figures became Khidr in the company of the *khayyál*, the Turkish mounted police, smart in khaki uniforms with red tarbooshes on their heads. At first it appeared that Khidr was in some sort of trouble and under the custody of the officers. Graham must have realized this was not the case—that the police were there for some other purpose—for I was standing close to him and felt his body tense.

The police rode up to us, but Khidr, looking rather smug, hung back. The younger officer appeared puzzled, as though he had expected dangerous brigands instead of the motley and harmless-appearing group before him, but the older of the two, a lieutenant, was prepared to do his duty and, drawing himself up, asked in heavily accented English, "Which of you is Louvois?"

Hakki bravely stepped forward. "I am the leader of this tour, and it is I who am responsible for its members. If you have anything to say, it must be said to me."

The lieutenant, while not intimidated, recognized Hakki's courage, for his tone became less belligerent. "Very well," he answered. "I have information that this Louvois has purchased valuable pieces of ancient art that he plans to remove from our country. Such behavior is illegal, and he must come with us to Antioch and face the authorities."

Hardly breathing, poor Monsieur Louvois stood quite still in the hope that he would somehow go unobserved, but a word or two from Khidr directed the soldier's attention to the proper target. The lieutenant snatched Monsieur Louvois's case from him and, forcing it open, clumsily began to unwrap the pieces inside. For a moment I believed Monsieur Louvois would choke the man. He must have thought again, for he remained where he was until the lieutenant discovered the ibex and began to handle it roughly.

Monsieur Louvois grabbed the officer's arm. *"Barbares!"* he shouted. "You know nothing of such things. Let them go where they are honored."

The lieutenant began to hustle the Frenchman off. "You will come with us to Antioch."

Sheikh Abd el Rehman thrust himself between the officer

and Monsieur Louvois. "This man has been a guest at my house. He has eaten my food. By custom he remains under my protection for three days." Monsieur Louvois, like a dog who knows his master, moved closer to the sheikh.

The lieutenant swung his rifle into position. The younger soldier looked like an innocent pedestrian who had wandered by mistake into a street brawl. The sheikh, ignoring the rifle, unsheathed his dagger. Hakki bravely stepped between them. "We must have no bloodshed," he pleaded in an unsteady voice. "There must be no violence, for that would be fatal to our party. We appreciate your kindness, sheikh, but Monsieur Louvois is under my protection and it is I who must decide what is to be done."

Hakki appeared to consider matters and then said, "Clearly Monsieur Louvois has broken the law." Paul Louvois shot him a furious look. Hakki went on. "I don't believe it is a serious offense; however, he must not remain here but be transfered to Antioch at once. That way we will not be separated from him by any distance. As soon as we reach Antioch, I will get in touch with the French consul, who will make everything right. But let the police know I hold them responsible for his treatment."

Hakki was now clearly in command of things. Watching him, I could not help wondering if he had more influence with the Turkish officers than we had guessed.

As the soldiers approached Monsieur Louvois, he shrank from them. Desperately he pulled a handful of money from his pocket and held it out to them, saying, "I'll pay a fine. You have only to tell me the amount; but you must leave the case with me." While the younger soldier looked hungrily at the money, the lieutenant hustled Monsieur Louvois away.

When they were gone, Father said, "Louvois was a fool not to have waited until he was alone with the officers. He offended them by offering a bribe in plain sight of everyone. Under those circumstances they could not possibly have accepted it. He was mistaken to think he could get out of this without giving up his treasures. The police will keep them to resell, and take the profit for themselves."

Hakki was upbraiding Khidr, who listened impassively until Hakki paused for breath, leaving him the opportunity to reply in a spiteful voice, "You expect us dragomen and mukaris to be honest, but these infidels you try to protect come here to break our laws. That man did what he should not do. Does he not deserve to be punished?" He turned on his heel and, mounting his horse, rode off after the policemen and their prisoner.

Edith apologized to Hakki, "You hired that rogue,

Khidr, on my say-so; I'm most awfully sorry. He must have looked into Louvois's saddlebag while we were in the orchard and seen the chance of a rich reward. I promise you there was no trouble when I traveled with him before, but of course he knew my things were not worth the having: dead plants and handfuls of seeds. We'll all march over to the French consul when we get to Antioch and straighten things out."

Father said, "I don't suppose he'll get into too much trouble, since he hasn't as yet actually taken the things out of Syria. But he won't be happy to leave his knickknacks behind." Father could not hide his satisfaction. "At least he will be too much in the eye of the authorities to do any business for the French."

Edith appeared shocked. "You mean it isn't just dirty old toys he's after?"

"Does anyone come to this country without some purpose?" I asked.

Graham said unkindly, "Are you suggesting the ideal state is to have no purpose?"

I gave Graham a hurt look.

"As there is no hotel in Antioch," Hakki said, "Watson and Sons has engaged rooms for us at the house of the British consul. He will surely know how to approach the French consul."

Father was doubtful. "I wouldn't be too optimistic about the abilities of the British consul in Antioch. I don't suppose the Foreign Office has been able to find an Englishman of any great ability who would be willing to settle in that god-forsaken place."

Graham pointed out, "Having traveled in Louvois's company, we will all be under a cloud."

I said, "Now that Monsieur Louvois has been arrested, I suppose we will all be closely watched. What will our reception be in Antioch?" I was afraid for Graham.

Graham said, "I suppose it won't be quite as nasty as the punishment meted out by Baybars during the Crusades, when sixteen thousand crusaders were butchered in Antioch."

"If you are counting bodies," Edith said with a sniff, "don't forget what the crusaders did to the Muslims and Jews in Jerusalem. There was quite a pile of arms and legs scattered about."

I winced, determined to ask no more questions.

❧

XVI

ANTIOCH

*I*N MY CONCERN FOR Monsieur Louvois and worry about Graham, I hardly noticed the dusty roads and the countryside through which we rode. On one side the city was sheltered by Mount Silpius; on the other side the Orontes River, like a fat snake, coiled and looped about the city.

The small village with its humble, windowless houses, stingy streets, and groves of mulberry and olive trees was hard to imagine as the city Hakki described as once having been the glory of Greece and Rome. Only the ancient wall, curving protectively around the town and stretching out onto the plain as far as you could see, suggested that Antioch had been worth defending. I was becoming depressed by all the dwindled cities, their glory gone to rags and tatters.

Hakki called to Mustafa, "You must take us to the home of the British consul." Mustafa led the caravan through quiet streets—for it was the hour of *kef*, the noon rest hour—to a house considerably larger than its modest neighbors. A servant with a tumble of curls and dressed in a fez, shirred trousers, silk shirt, embroidered vest, and a brightly striped sash opened the door and led us into a handsome drawing room. There was a haughty quality about the servant's courtesy that suggested we were lucky indeed to enjoy his attentions. With a toss of his curls he asked us to wait while he summoned his master.

Seen from the street, the house showed nothing but a few narrow slits serving as windows, so I was astonished by my first view of its interior. The walls were hung with silk prayer rugs and the floors laid with Turkish carpets in rich colors. There was the shine of polished brass, and everywhere there were tiles decorated in bright blue. In my grimy clothes I felt out of place, but the consul, who hurried into the room to welcome us, immediately set about making us feel at home. He was a small, immaculately dressed man in his early fifties wearing a neat gray suit and an impeccable shirt with a stiff collar.

His approach to us was motherly. "You must tell me what refreshments we can bring you. When I am riding in this terrible countryside, which I do as seldom as possible, I always fancy a glass of lemonade. How would that do? And as soon as you have had some refreshments, we'll get you baths. You look rather hot and you certainly need dusting. Now, do stop standing about as though this were a garden party at Buckingham Palace."

He urged us onto chairs made comfortable with silk cushions and directed his servant with the Medusa curls, who hovered in the background, to bring lemonade and meringues. The latter treat seemed a wild luxury, and in spite of our worry about Monsieur Louvois I saw that we were all beginning to relax, thinking we were in the hands of someone resourceful.

"Now you must tell me your names," the consul said. "I am Cornelius Robinson, England's humble representative in this very humble town. Was I misinformed, or was I to have the pleasure of accommodating five guests? Have you been careless and misplaced someone?"

Hakki launched into the tale of Monsieur Louvois's arrest, ending with "We hoped you might give us help."

Mr. Robinson was distressed. "Of course I and Monsieur Potton, who is the consular agent for France, will do all we can, but the truth is our influence here is rather disappointing. It is a Turkish city, and I suspect they will be tempted to make a great deal of the matter. I don't suppose a long prison sentence is in the offing, but possibly some sort of slap on the hand and certainly deportation and a rather heavy fine. Even a single day in a prison here is unwholesome, if not actually hideous, so we will put a stop to that. The sooner we make an effort, the better. Saladin will show you to your rooms, which I'm afraid are very modest, and I will go at once to the French consul. Any of you with influence might come along."

Father said, "I don't have much influence—I'm only a solicitor—but I'll put in a word for Louvois."

Edith offered herself. "I'm not sure I can do much, but the Turks will be so shocked to have a woman on the attack, it might bring them to their senses."

The room assigned to Edith and me was small but full of charming touches. The draperies on the windows and the bed hangings were of a heavy pale-peach silk. Silken pillows in pastel colors were thrown on the bed, and on the floor was a Turkish rug in rich shades of apricot and brown. I lay down, thinking I would rest a moment or two while Edith went with Father and Mr. Robinson to the French consul. The next thing I knew was the sound of knocking. Graham was at my door.

He wanted forgiveness. "I feel a coward for not going along with the others," he said, "but there is something about this moldering city that frightens me: Anyone might be bought or sold here. Look what happened to Louvois. I'm afraid I could be next, and I don't have the courage to put myself in the lions' den. If they got hold of me and used torture, I'm not sure I would be up to keeping quiet about the tribes I've made contact with."

Graham seemed truly frightened, like a small boy who has been caught with his hand in the cookie jar. I felt a great tenderness for him and reached out my hand in sympathy or something more. He took my hand and brought it to his lips. "Can I count on you to stand by me?" he said. "I feel the others on the trip would not be sorry to see me follow Louvois to a Turkish jail."

"I'm sure that's not true, but of course you can count on me," I said. I believed there was nothing I wouldn't do to protect Graham.

We heard voices in the rooms below and hurriedly went downstairs, to find Father, the consul, and Edith, all looking glum.

"Poor beggar," Father said. "They've got him cooped up in a filthy hole with some cutthroats to keep him company. I've never seen anyone so miserable."

Mr. Robinson said, "The French consul is trying the informal connections he has in the city. We went on to visit the Turkish authorities, where Miss Phillips played a part.

Quite intimidated they were by her, even allowed her a private talk with the official in charge. I believe your father did some good as well, Miss Hamilton. He also had a private talk with the Turkish official. What a mysterious group you are with all your secrets!

"Now we must have our dinner. You are all probably hungry for a meal at a table. I have never understood why people will pay to wander about in the desert and be uncomfortable. If you would like to retire to your rooms to wash up, I'll see to the cuisine."

In my room Saladin brought warm water for our washstand and then bowed himself out, seeming less a servant than an actor in a play of his own imagining. "An odd fellow, that," Edith said.

"He goes nicely with the decoration," I said.

"A little too much the poseur for my taste," said Edith. "I don't know where to sit or stand in this room—the carpet looks too valuable to tread on with my boots, and the pillows and draperies are something out of a harem. Whatever Robinson says, I'm afraid I feel more at home in a tent; at least there you know where you are."

But for all her protestations Edith put on her one good dress for dinner. "You look quite smart," I said.

"Nonsense. It's just that it's been a week since you've

seen me with my face properly washed. You, on the other hand, are quite lovely."

I had dug out a sky-blue silk skirt-and-waist and was feeling festive. "What I really wish I could wear are those draperies. What a stunning gown they would make."

Saladin ushered us into the dining room. Porcelain plates rimmed in gold, and knives and forks of hammered brass and silver, were set out on a gleaming mahogany table. There were thick damask napkins with patterns of leaping stags woven though them and candlesticks of cut glass. Saladin, passing the dishes, looked as amused as ever, as if at any moment he would give up the game of waiting on us and sit down at the table beside his master.

We were served grilled lamb perfectly roasted and aubergines done in a spicy sauce. For dessert there was a compote of exotic fruits, and with coffee the meringues reappeared. In spite of the excellent dinner we were all tired and relieved to hear Graham excuse himself: "I'm afraid the long journey and our concern for Louvois, to say nothing of the effect of all that excellent food, has made me sleepy." In minutes the dinner party was over.

It is hard to keep on worrying when the worry is not about yourself, but about someone else. At breakfast, after our night's sleep, we were more lively and optimistic, each of us with some idea of how we might rescue Monsieur Louvois. We were comparing ideas as we finished bowls of fresh strawberries, when there was a knocking on the outer door. Saladin led Monsieur Louvois into the dining room. Even in the desert he had always been carefully dressed, so it was shocking to see him unshaven and in wrinkled and soiled clothes. I noticed with surprise that he still had his case. From the way he clutched it, the precious antiquities appeared still to be there. He looked quickly about the room. "I see you have had a little more luxury than I have had." His voice was bitter.

Mr. Robinson, all concern, was on his feet at once. "Welcome, welcome. I am delighted to have you with us. Please join us for breakfast, or would you prefer to go upstairs first and change?"

Louvois looked longingly at the table, but he said, "I must bathe and then *je regrette* I must go. I'm afraid I am persona non grata in this city, and I have no wish to involve the rest of you. I only wanted to say *merci beaucoup* for your help in having me released. I leave tomorrow from Alexandretta, and the Turks have kindly insisted on seeing me there themselves." He gave one more envious look at the table—was unable to resist the plucking and consuming of a strawberry—then hurried away after Saladin.

Edith watched Monsieur Louvois's departure. "I'd say he was in a bit of a rush."

"I can assure you," Mr. Robinson said, "that after a few hours in a Turkish prison, one would wish to leave the Ottoman Empire as soon as possible. However, relieved as I am, I'm surprised they've given him his freedom so quickly."

Before we left the breakfast table, Monsieur Louvois was back—scrubbed, in fresh clothes, and ready to depart. Even under the circumstances his leave-taking was abrupt. There were handshakes for the men and kisses on the hand for me and a startled Edith. "I am most sorry to have caused trouble for our little *famille*," he said. In a moment his carriage had drawn up, and with a quick wave Paul Louvois, still hugging his case, was gone.

"How do you suppose he managed to get out of prison with all his possessions?" Graham asked the consul.

"There's no telling. I wish I could take some credit for his release," Mr. Robinson answered, "but I should be less than honest if I did, and the French consular agent is a man of even less influence. I do not think money alone could have been successful in releasing him, but perhaps I underestimated the amount at his disposal. Or perhaps Louvois had something beside money to offer the police?" He paused to study us. "I don't suppose he was privy to any particular information that might be useful to the Turkish authorities?"

"I can't think of any information he might have," Edith said, "unless the Turkish police would be interested in a lecture on early Assyrian art."

I could not help looking across the table at Graham. His face had gone pale beneath its tan, and a fine perspiration had broken out across his forehead. I knew what he was thinking: Monsieur Louvois had a great deal of information about him if he chose to use it. He also had information about Father. I looked at Father, but he appeared unconcerned.

"Now that you have been freed from your worry about Monsieur Louvois, let me make a few suggestions for your visit here in Antioch." Mr. Robinson assumed the attitude of the conscientious host. Hakki looked put out at the consul's taking over his duties, Father was paying no attention at all, and Graham appeared lost in worried thought. Only Edith and I half listened to what seemed a well-rehearsed speech.

"Our village was called by Marcellinus 'the fair crown of the Orient.' Antony married Cleopatra here. You will know from your New Testament that Peter was in Antioch, as, of course, was Paul. I don't suppose you want to view our meager industries—licorice and knives and very good soap; I use it myself." His lecture was interrupted by a pounding on the door. "Good heavens, what now? I've never known my place to be the center of so much excitement."

For a moment I thought Monsieur Louvois had returned. Instead it was a contingent of Turkish soldiers whose number overwhelmed the small room. Instinctively our little group drew together. Mr. Robinson stood up from the table. "I do not know why I should put up with this trespass," he said. This was bold of him, for the soldiers were armed and looked determined.

The *bashi*, or major, who led the group insinuated himself forward in a catlike movement. He was slender and wiry, with long sleek mustaches that enclosed his chin in a kind of parentheses, and a red line across his forehead where, before he removed it in deference to his surroundings, his fez had rested. "We regret this intrusion, Consul, but we are here to take a Mr. Graham Geddes away with us on a charge of spying." The word *spying* terrified me, and I dug my fingers into my father's arm and held on. Father's hand covered mine.

"You must be joking. You can't do that. I'm a British subject." Graham looked toward the window as if he might be considering leaping to freedom. I prayed he wouldn't do anything that might cause the soldiers to draw their guns and shoot him. I was terrified for Graham, but I was sure that any words on my part would only lead to more trouble.

With the greatest difficulty I kept silent, but I resolved that if the soldiers took him, wherever he was, I would find him.

In an incriminating voice the major addressed Graham. "We know of the villages in which you have sown seeds of discontent with our government and our sultan, trying to foment revolution. You were not acting then like a British subject, and so we will not treat you like one." He grabbed Graham's arm.

Mr. Robinson said, "I absolutely forbid you to lay your hands on that man while he is on British territory."

The major's answer was to approach Graham with his hand on his holster. "I do not believe the British government will raise many objections," the officer said. "It is our understanding that this man's activities have not been in the interest of the British government."

Hakki got to his feet and, catching at one of Graham's arms, tried to free him from the bashi's grip. The bashi pulled Hakki away. "We have much room in our Antioch jail, and if there is any further interference with our duty, we can make another offender quite comfortable there." The next minute Graham was marched out of the house.

I was shaking. My hands were ice cold. "How could you let them take him?" I asked. "Why didn't someone stop them?" But even as I made the accusations, I knew there was nothing they could have done, and I was ashamed of taking my fear out on them.

"Mohammed could have given Geddes away," Edith said. "If the Turks caught up with him in the desert, they would certainly have found a way to get him to tell what he and Geddes were up to."

Looking puzled, Mr. Robinson said, "I'm afraid I am in the dark. Is there something I should know?"

"You might as well be aware of what we're up against." Father's voice was impatient. He was going over too-familiar territory. "Geddes, I'm afraid, is guilty of just what he is accused of. I don't believe he meant any great harm, but the truth is he belongs to a secret society composed of the revolutionary Young Turks, whose plan it is to depose the present sultan and restore constitutional government to Turkey. Graham tried to enlist the sympathy of the Druze tribes. He went about promising them that under the new Turkish government they would be given a certain measure of self-rule. Not only the Druzes, but any group under the heel of Turkey."

Edith was indignant. "That was very wrong of Geddes. I've never thought one ought to meddle in the affairs of another country; there is in one's own country confusion enough."

Mr. Robinson looked thoughtful. "Did your Louvois know about Graham?"

"I'm sure he guessed," Father said. "He wasn't one to miss much. I see. You are suggesting Louvois gave them damming information on Geddes in exchange for his own release. Not a very nice thought."

"Geddes is certainly a much bigger fish for the Turks, with his involvement in the Young Turks' revolution," Mr. Robinson said.

I had seen the hunger in Monsieur Louvois's eyes when he'd looked at his treasures and the tenderness with which he handled them. "What can we do?" I asked. "It isn't just the horror of prison, is it? It might be worse than that." I was thinking of what my father said about the "methods" that might have been used on Mohammed, and how Graham had worried about what he might say under torture.

Mr. Robinson reached across the table and patted my hand. "There is no need to think of unpleasant things. I will telegraph Britain's diplomatic offices in Beirut at once. Just for a bit we won't mention to them what Geddes has been up to. I suspect they would not be overly sympathetic to Geddes's cause if they knew an Englishman was riding up and down the countryside opposing England's policies."

Edith said, "What we have to do is to work out a plan

and write it down on paper, step by step. That's the orderly way. First, Robinson will telegraph Beirut. Certainly we should talk with the *kaimakam*, Antioch's governor. What else is to be done?"

In this way a plan was put together and, to humor Edith, written down like a shopping list. All the while I was thinking of Graham in a Turkish prison. I had no confidence in their schemes. I knew that I must find Graham at once; that if only I could see him, he would tell me what I must do to rescue him. Saying I would feel better if I lay down for a while, I excused myself.

I headed for the stairway, but as soon as I was out of sight, I escaped from the house. Hurrying down the street, I hailed a carriage, telling the driver to take me to the army garrison. He looked skeptical, shaking his head. "*Effendim*, no lady goes there. Only soldiers."

"I must see someone there. It is very important that I go as quickly as possible." Finally, after some urging and considerable baksheesh, he did as I asked. From the carriage window the city appeared shabby. A threat seemed to lurk around every corner. I wanted to tell Graham that I finally understood what he and the Young Turks were trying to do. This was a country where soldiers came into your house and took you away. If you weren't important—if, like

Mohammed, you did not have consuls and foreign offices to look after you—you were never seen again.

I kept leaning over to urge the driver to go more quickly. "*Effendim*, I go as quick as I can," he said. Clearly he thought I was mad and was weighing the danger to himself should he assist me in some rash action. When we reached the garrison, the driver was reluctant to let me get out of the carriage. "Turkish soldiers here. No place for you," he said. When I handed him his money, he counted it twice, trusting me in nothing. I asked him to wait and he nodded, but he was already snapping the reins, anxious to be rid of the mad girl. By the time I reached the garrison entrance, the carriage was out of sight.

The garrison was a modest one, the barracks no more than a jumble of small stables and buildings. I chose a building whose windows were barred. I began to hurry—sure now that Graham was being held there, I was desperate to see him. I knocked on the door with so much force, I bruised my knuckles. An officer pulled the door open, startling me, and I saw it was the major who had carried Graham away. He was as taken aback as I was.

"I must see Mr. Geddes," I insisted.

"Impossible. He goes to Alexandretta."

"What will happen to him?"

"They will put him on a boat for Istanbul, nothing more." He looked over his shoulder toward a dark hallway and then back at me. I thought I saw a glimmer of pity in his eyes. "Go away quickly; you will only make trouble for him." As hard as it was to leave without seeing Graham, I believed the officer. If what they wished was merely to get Graham out of the country as quietly as possible, any disturbance I made would complicate things. With reluctance I allowed the major to guide me out of the building and find a carriage for me.

As the carriage was passing through the center of the city, I saw Monsieur Louvois sitting at a café. Immediately I shouted to the driver to stop. My voice was so frantic, when he reined in the horses it nearly upset us. Flinging coins his way, I jumped out into the street, where a little knot of men gathered to see what I would do next. When Monsieur Louvois looked up to find me at his table, he appeared pleased; then, as he read the anger on my face, he looked about him for some escape.

I stood over him, not caring who saw or heard me. "How could you do that to Graham?" I accused Louvois. "How could you betray him? He's imprisoned in the garrison and they're taking him to Istanbul. He might be shot as a spy!"

"*Ma chère* Julia, lower your voice. Everyone is looking

at us. Whatever can you mean? I know nothing about Graham."

"It's perfectly obvious. You told the Turkish authorities that Graham was a member of the Young Turks so they would arrest him and let you go."

"That is preposterous! For me it was just a matter of getting through to the French government. Monsieur Potton managed for me. My country acted at once." Monsieur Louvois appeared genuinely shocked at my accusation.

"Why would the French government be so quick to help you when you've broken the laws of this country?"

"After what has happened, I believe I can tell you I am not altogether the fool you take me for. France is as interested in Syria as Britain is—and has a greater right to it. It is true that I collect antiquities, but I also keep an eye open for France, and in return my country helps with my collecting when help is needed. It is a useful partnership. Fortunately, their influence here is quite strong. But I see from your face you are not entirely surprised by my secret tasks. Perhaps your father guessed? He seems to have much information for a solicitor."

"Yes. He knew you had some connection with the French government. But why did you hurry away from the consul's house so quickly, and what are you doing here?"

"My transportation to Alexandretta does not leave until later today. I am just biding my time. I went away from Robinson's because I felt embarrassed by what had happened: I had given everyone much trouble. But for your traitor you must look elsewhere."

I believed him. "I'm sorry, Monsieur Louvois. I've made a mistake. I hope you get home safely." All the way back I tried to tell myself that it must have been Mohammed, that it could not have been my father who had betrayed Graham—but I couldn't be sure.

They were all waiting for me. "Where the devil did you go?" Father demanded.

"I went to see Graham," I said. I was too exhausted for anything but the truth.

"That was a stupid and dangerous thing to do." Father's face was white, and a blue vein in his forehead throbbed.

Mr. Robinson greeted my story of Graham's imminent departure for Alexandretta and Istanbul with little surprise. "They won't want to deal with him here in Syria. In Istanbul the sultan's men will hope to hear about his connections. I suspect he will tell them, for they can be very persuasive."

My heart sank. They had deceived me at the garrison. Graham would be sent to Alexandretta and then Istanbul, only to meet with further imprisonment and torture.

Father, calmer now but still furious with me, said, "Julia, you were very foolish. They might have suspected you of having something to do with Geddes and taken you as well."

Edith agreed. "Your father is quite right. You must stay away from Geddes; the man is a fool. There is no one more dangerous than someone who has set out to save the world."

Mr. Robinson was slower to agree. "I quite see that this Geddes is foolish, but he doesn't sound dangerous."

"He's not," I said, relieved to have someone on Graham's side. "And he's not foolish, only determined. He has been risking his life to help others: This is not even his country."

"That is exactly the point I was making," Edith said.

"Julia, you are talking about things of which you are totally ignorant," Father scolded me.

Mr. Robinson must have felt he was surrounded by a swarm of wasps. He announced, "Really, you must all calm down. I hope you won't mind if I tag along to Alexandretta with you tomorrow. I have some business there with our vice-consul, and I may be of some use. In the meantime I can give you the name of a man who has excellent carriages for hire." He reverted to his maternal tone. "Also, you must all be sure to take your quinine, three grains at the very least. Malaria is everywhere in Alexandretta. A dangerous city."

I knew my father wanted to get me alone so he could have at me for trying to see Graham. To avoid that, I stayed on with Mr. Robinson and Edith, who got into a discussion of the flora of Aleppo. Finally, Father and Edith went off to their rooms, and Mr. Robinson and I were left to ourselves.

"You said my father had a private chat with the Turkish official when you saw him about Monsieur Louvois. Father could have betrayed Graham to get Louvois off and Graham out of the way."

A raised eyebow was the only surprise Mr. Robinson showed at my accusation. After a moment he said, "In my early days with the Foreign Office in London, I seem to have heard of a Carlton Hamilton on the Arab Desk. I never met the man, but I believe he had something to do with scotching a request I had put in for a post in Morocco. I don't suppose there is any connection between that man and your father?" I said nothing. "Well, of course I understand why someone from the Foreign Office would want to keep his identity quiet: Just now Turkey is not too fond of us Englishmen."

The consul lowered his voice. "I wonder if your father doesn't also disapprove of the amount of time you spend with Geddes?"

I looked away. "I don't think Father would betray Graham for me, but he might for England."

"I have tried to reason things out," Mr. Robinson said. "First, your father was made ill in some way, and in that way the mukari Mohammed was exposed. Louvois was arrested and now Geddes has been betrayed. I think all of these things must be connected, but I can't decide who among you would do such things. It's most intriguing. For now you must get a good night's sleep, and we'll see what is to be done when we get to Alexandretta tomorrow."

There was no sleep for thinking of Graham. Edith, hearing me toss and turn, sat up in bed and read in an instructive voice a verse from the Koran: "'Of his mercy God hath made for you the night that ye may rest. . . .'" Toward dawn, with the raucous cry of ravens for a lullaby, I drifted off to an hour of restless sleep and nightmares of foundering ships.

XVII

ALEXANDRETTA

W E LEFT FOR ALEXANDRETTA in the morning. Father insisted that I be placed in his carriage. "I suppose you're keeping an eye on me," I accused him.

In an impatient voice Father said, "Since I am no longer able to imagine what you might do next, I have no alternative." When Mr. Robinson joined us, a shadow of irritation passed over Father's face, but ever the diplomat, he greeted the consul cordially. Saladin sat with the driver while Hakki and Edith traveled in a second carriage.

I twisted around to look at Antioch's vanishing outline. "Do you think they've already taken Graham to Alexandretta?" I asked Mr. Robinson. I hated the idea of leaving him behind in Antioch.

"Oh, they would have been off first thing this morning," the consul said. "His guards would be anxious for a few extra hours in Alexandretta: It is a more exciting town than Antioch."

It was a long day's journey from Antioch to the sea. At first there were only hints of water: streams flowing into marshes and marshes fanning into deltas; then, as we made our way down the foothills, the Mediterranean stretched out in front of us, a blue dream after so many days of dusty dryness. There was a freshness in the air all the way to Alexandretta, where we found the harbor crowded with boats, caiques, and dhows in every shape and size, their sails flapping in the wind like a flock of jumbled birds.

"Odd as it may seem, when one thinks of the desert," Mr. Robinson said, "the Arabs were once great sailors."

It was one of his many attempts on the trip to make polite conversation. Like earlier attempts it was met with a polite "Quite" from Father and silence from me, for I was concentrating on the three steamers I saw anchored in the harbor.

Suddenly afraid, I asked Mr. Robinson, "I don't suppose you have any idea when Graham's boat will sail?"

"We consuls always know the schedules of the steamers. If they are taking Geddes to Istanbul, he will probably leave on the *Poseidon*, which sails tomorrow afternoon for Athens, with a stop on the way at Mersina in Turkey. Your own steamer sails for Istanbul the following day."

The carriages pulled up in front of a hotel with patched

brickwork and cracked window glass. When I had him alone for a moment, I asked my father, "Won't you tell the Turkish authorities about your position with the Foreign Office? Surely you have enough influence to help Graham."

"I can't do that," Father said. "I'm under orders. Divulging my identity would be a breach of security, although the Turks may soon know of it."

"What do you mean?"

"Geddes has been discreet up to now, but let's see how he manages to keep secrets with the Turks asking questions."

I thought this heartless. "But isn't that all the more reason to get him away from the Turks, to keep him from exposing you? Surely you can do something."

"I'll see the British consul here in Alexandretta. If he appears trustworthy, I might say a word or two, but I must be convinced that my identity won't get passed on to the Turks. If they had absolute knowledge of my connection with the Foreign Office and my mission here, they would come down on the Foreign Office in a way that would put England in an awkward position."

I gave my father a hard look. "Better on England than Graham."

Father appeared shocked.

Hakki arranged to have tea served in the hotel parlor, a dark room crowded with too much furniture and smelling of Turkish cigarettes. I sank down onto a lumpy chair and choked on the tea's cloying blend of mint and sugar. I heard myself saying in an accusing voice, "I don't know how we can sit here drinking tea like a lot of stupid British tourists when Graham is a prisoner."

"But we are British tourists, my dear," Father said.

Hakki, in a show of sympathy, passed me some sticky bits of pastry. To cover my misery, I nibbled one. It tasted of rosewater, and flakes of the pastry glued themselves to my fingers. As I reached for my napkin, I caught Mr. Robinson looking at me with so knowing a look that I flushed. It was a look that signaled conspiracy against my father. I guessed that the consul was at war with my father for his old grievance and was seeking to enlist me in that war.

Edith, who had been watching all of us with an amused look, pushed back her chair and got to her feet. "I for one intend to take a bit of a rest before I begin packing for the steamer."

"There is no need to hurry with your packing," Hakki said, eager to prolong his tea party, where everyone was under his eye. "Our luggage will not be collected until tomorrow evening."

I went to my room pretending fatigue and was relieved to find I had a room to myself. I tried to think what I must do, for I had no faith in my father's offer to help Graham. The walls in the hotel were thin, and Edith's gentle wheezes coming from the next room distracted me so that I found myself waiting for each successive breath, as if a life depended on it. I wanted to concentrate on Graham, to think of a way to free him. Like the consul, I was beginning to be sure there was someone determined to do us harm.

There was a subdued knock at my door, and opening it, I found Mr. Robinson. Half watchful, half curious, the consul glanced around the room. "Forgive me for invading your quarters. I thought you might be interested to know that I had guessed correctly and Geddes is to sail on the *Poseidon*."

"How did you find out?"

"I have friends in odd places here in Alexandretta."

"Do you think my father can do anything for Graham?"

"I don't know that he wishes to do anything. I tried to go along with him to the office of Alexandretta's British consul and found that your father did not welcome my company. He disapproves of me. In spite of the fact that the consul, Haversham, is a friend of mine, your father indicated I would be a hindrance rather than a help, but I think it is more than that. At any rate, how far are you prepared to go to rescue your friend?"

"I would do anything."

I saw that he believed me. "I have a rather spiteful desire to give your father trouble. I've seen too many of his kind in the Foreign Office: smug men who think they know what is best for the world. Mind you, I believe your friend Geddes, with his playing about with the Young Turks and his mad ideas of subverting the Ottoman Empire, is just as bother-some, but he didn't strike me as being as arrogant and patronizing as your father. I hope you don't mind my speaking of your father this way, but I'd rather like to foil his little plan, whatever that may be." He gave me an impish wink.

Whatever my own doubts about my father, I did not like hearing those suspicions from someone else. It made me feel small and disloyal. "It couldn't have been Father who betrayed Graham."

"That doesn't mean he wouldn't be delighted to take advantage of Geddes's misfortune. Now I had best leave. I no longer hear Miss Phillips's puffs and sputters, and we don't want me seen sidling out of your room. I expect your father will be returning shortly, and we will make our plans after we hear from him."

Edith opened her door to see Mr. Robinson leaving. She

hurried into my room. She must have been a busy sleeper, for her hair stood out at odd angles.

"I hope Robinson wasn't encouraging you to do anything foolish?" Edith said. "I've marked him as a mischief-maker. You had best let Geddes be; I'm sure the Turks will turn him over to the British authorities once they get him to Istanbul."

It was exactly what Father said later, when he returned and joined me on the hotel veranda. I had turned eagerly toward him. "What did you find out?"

"I had a most useful talk with Haversham, who is the British consul here. He has been in touch with Istanbul. Our people there will meet the *Poseidon* when it arrives and collect Geddes. There's no point in your being concerned any further. I think Robinson was a little put out because I didn't see fit to take him along; probably thought I was going over his head, but I can't think Robinson is one of the Foreign Office favorites."

I couldn't help asking, "Will we see Graham when we get to Istanbul?"

"I shouldn't count on it. Even though his ship sails tomorrow afternoon and ours doesn't leave until the next morning, his ship, the *Poseidon*, has a twenty-four hour layover in Mersina."

"I thought we were going to spend a few days in Istanbul."

"I know I promised them to you, but I heard from Haversham there has been a little skirmish in Morocco that threatens to involve Spain and France, so I must get back to the Foreign Office. I seem to recall Robinson in his younger days wanting a post in Morocco. Lucky for Morocco I kept that from going through. The man is better off where he can't do much harm."

Father advised, "Put any worries about Geddes out of your head, Julia, and enjoy your last day in the Levant. I would, however, suggest you stay close to the hotel: This town is most unhealthy—leprosy in ancient times, malaria now, as you can see from the yellow complexion of the local citizenry."

While Father went to dress for dinner, I remained on the hotel veranda looking out at the ring of hills circling the unhealthy town. A month before, I would have given years of my life to experience the view before me at that moment—the ancient town, the parade of exotically dressed people looking like an opera director's fantasy, the mingled smells of jasmine and spices and other things not quite so pleasant. Now I could think only of Graham. I felt uneasy about my father's reassurances. Although I did not believe he would purposely lie to me, I suspected he was keeping something back as one colors what one tells a child in proportion to what one thinks a child can understand.

I could not guess what Graham would do if he were released. When he returned to England and Oxford, would he think of me, or would he consider my world, as I was beginning to, pinched and dull? And how would I ever be able to return to that world of Durham Place?

"Julia, I've been looking for you." Mr. Robinson, obviously out of breath, dropped into a chair next to me. He was a short man, and as he settled back, his shoes barely touched the floor. Looking about first to be sure we were alone, he asked, "Have you spoken with your father?"

"Yes. He said Graham will be released to someone from the British Foreign Office when the *Poseidon* docks at Istanbul."

"Ah, well, that won't do Geddes much good," Robinson said.

"What do you mean?" My distrust of my father returned.

"My servant, Saladin, has been rather busy. I sent him to talk with some of the crew on the *Poseidon*. He knows his way around the wharves and was able to find out that an Englishman has already been placed on board and is guarded by Turkish officers. Unquestionably it is Geddes. The guards will whisk Geddes off the boat when it stops in Mersina. When it arrives in Istanbul, Geddes will not be on it."

"Why Mersina?"

"The Turks have no intention of handing Geddes over to the British in Istanbul; they feel he has useful information about the Young Turks that they mean to have."

"Was my father lying to me?" I was not sure I was asking the right person.

"We mustn't think that." Robinson frowned and pursed his lips in an attitude of mock concentration. "No, I suspect it was Bunny Haversham, the British consul, here in Alexandretta. One always likes to think that one's consul is on one's side. Unfortunately that is not always the case with Haversham. He is what your Louvois would call an *homme d'affaires*—a man of affairs. He has a little import-export thing going for him in addition to his consular duties— strictly against Foreign Office rules, of course. Without the blessing of the Turks he is out of business. Naturally, if they asked him to mislead your father, he would do so—reluctantly, of course; the man is not altogether bad. But your father could not have known all that."

"Why would England keep a man like Haversham on?" I asked.

"He is very good at his job and they don't know about his second profession. But that is not the question you really wish to ask."

"What can we can do to help Graham?"

"I have a plan. Just now Saladin is attempting a friendship with one of the guards on the *Poseidon*. Let us see how that progresses. I'll contact you in the morning. In the meantime I would not discuss any of this with your father. Either he will not believe me or he will make a good deal of trouble for Haversham, who happens to be a friend of mine, and one doesn't have too many of those hereabouts. Also, we may have to take some steps that your father would find troubling, and we don't want him interfering." He gave my hand a reassuring pat and left me.

Neither Edith nor Mr. Robinson appeared for dinner, leaving Father and me to eat alone. The food was a miserable hodgepodge of what the hotel assumed the British preferred: dry, overdone meat and rocklike potatoes that resisted a fork. Alone at a dinner table with my father, I remembered all the morose, silent meals we had shared at Durham Place. Desperate for certainty, I blurted out, "Father, do you think Mr. Haversham is telling the truth?"

"I would certainly not make that assumption about Haversham. But what exactly do you mean?"

"I have heard, and I can't say where, that the Turks will take Graham off the ship, not at Istanbul but at Mersina."

Father looked startled. I couldn't tell whether he was surprised that he had been lied to or just surprised that I had learned the truth. "Who told you that?"

I shook my head.

"Never mind. I can guess. Robinson is a meddler; nevertheless, all my experience suggests that when there is a choice of what to believe, the more unpleasant possibility is apt to be the accurate one."

"Then you think Graham is in danger from the Turks?"

Father was silent for a long while, just looking intently at me. Finally he asked, "Would you care so much?"

I thought if ever there was a time for truth, it was now. "I would care a great deal."

Father looked down at his plate and, after a moment's consideration, pushed it away, his dinner nearly untouched. "I'll see what I can do tomorrow morning," he said. "Just promise me that you won't attempt anything foolish." At that moment the waiter came to the table to exclaim unhappily over the food remaining on our plates, relieving me of the need to make a promise I had no intention of keeping.

My room was stifling; even the airy mosquito netting

that muffled my bed seemed to keep out the air. In desperation I pushed the netting aside and went out onto my balcony. The dark city, Alexandretta, "little Alexandria," was sheltered by the foothills of the Taurus Mountains. Earlier I had watched the hills fade from emerald to jade to gray. Now they were nothing more than black shadows. Beyond those mountains lay Turkey and Mersina. I was sure that if the *Poseidon* sailed with Graham aboard, I would never see him again. Why, I wondered, did I have to depend on the consul and my father for everything; why could I do nothing for myself? But try as I might, I couldn't think what to do. As the night inched on, my ideas grew more desperate.

The next morning Mr. Robinson was back in my room before breakfast, a bulky carpetbag under his arm and a conspiratorial expression on his face. "I believe we can solve our problem if you are willing to take a risk." He studied me and must have felt reassured about my willingness, for he went on. "Saladin has managed to bribe one of two Turkish soldiers guarding Geddes's cabin on the *Poseidon*. The soldier will leave the door between Geddes's cabin and the adjoining cabin unlocked, but this will not permit Geddes to escape. Unfortunately, only one soldier is bribeable. The second soldier outside Geddes's cabin as well as the two soldiers on the gangplank would intercept him."

"But what can I do?"

"You will be an Arab woman on her way to Mersina to join her husband; Arab women take steamers to Mersina and Istanbul all the time. We have arranged that you are to have the cabin next to Graham, the one with the unlocked door."

"I have no Arab things to wear." I could not find my way into Robinson's plans, though I was excited, trusting his cunning.

"Saladin has gone to the bazaar and found you something."

The consul held out a long dark abeyah and veil like those worn by Arab women. Mr. Robinson watched my reaction with approval. "I see you are not afraid of taking a chance. I thought with a father as autocratic as yours, you might be less adventurous."

Now that I was about to disobey him, I felt I ought to defend my father. "He means well," I said, aware at once of what a feeble defense that was.

"I think he would not approve of my little plot, but he need never know. You are to make your way to Geddes's adjoining cabin. There you will give him this carpetbag, which contains clothes identical to yours, but in his size. Just before the *Poseidon* sails, Geddes will walk out of your cabin as a veiled Arab woman and go ashore. The soldiers at the gangplank will have no reason to be suspicious. Give Geddes enough time to get safely away and into a carriage that I will have waiting, and then, while our guard diverts his companion's attention, you will leave the ship in your own clothes. The soldiers at the gangplank will imagine you have been on board the ship to see off a fellow countryman."

"But my passage. They will want to see my ticket."

"That, too, has been taken care of. Here are papers of identification showing you to be an Arab woman, tickets for your passage to Mersina, and the reservation for the cabin next to Graham's."

I was grateful for his efforts, but I felt he was less interested in saving Graham than in heaping revenge on Father. For that, I felt sure, he wouldn't mind putting me in danger. I was sorry to be a part of his revenge, but not sorry enough to abandon Graham.

"When you have changed your clothes, leave by the back entrance of the hotel and you will be thought to be a servant. Be sure to have the driver drop you off out of sight of the wharf. The sort of Arab woman you are supposed to be would not arrive in a carriage. There is one pitfall, and it is a serious one. You don't speak Arabic, but that is a risk we must take. I don't believe anyone will address you—it is considered unseemly for a man to engage in conversation with a woman not of his family. If they do, you must pretend to be overcome with shyness. Just giggle. I don't like to send you on a mission that has its dangers, but Geddes would not trust a stranger. Of course you must not breathe a word to your father."

XVIII

THE IMPOSTOR

To show my gratitude to the consul, I reached for his hand, which was small and soft and slightly furry, so I felt I had gotten hold of a little timid animal. As soon as Mr. Robinson left, I began to struggle into the abeyah and veil. I was trying to arrange them in the way I had noticed on Arab women when Edith came into my room without knocking. In someone else that would have been considered rude, but in Edith it was only a brusqueness I had long since become used to, knowing it indicated nothing more than an impatience with social niceties.

"Good Lord! You would be the last person I would have thought of as going native. What are you doing in that costume?"

I was caught unawares, and anxious for help, I explained, "It's a disguise. Mr. Robinson has arranged for me to get into the cabin next to Graham's, and I'm to bring an

Arab woman's clothes to him so he can get off the boat. Promise not to breathe a word to Father."

I glanced at the mirror. "Edith, you know about these things—can you arrange the veil so it looks right? I'm too nervous to think about what I'm doing."

In an angry voice Edith said, "Robinson has no right to put you up to a trick like that. You are not playing a child's game, you know. You could be caught and carted off to a Turkish prison yourself."

"I'll be careful." I could not keep fear out of my voice.

"Nonsense. What if they ask you a question. You can't say more than 'please' and 'thank you' in Arabic. They'll spot you for an impostor immediately."

"Mr. Robinson said it was a risk, but he thought since I had papers and my passage, no one would question me." I was rapidly losing my resolve, and more to encourage myself than convince Edith, I said, "It's the only chance to get Graham off the boat."

Edith considered. "Look, here, I speak the language like a native. I'll do it for you, but you're to stay in your room until the thing is done, and you are not to say a word to Robinson. It was very good of him to manage all of this, and it wouldn't do to hurt his feelings by letting him know you have altered his little game without consulting him. I've seen the way he looks at your father. Obviously Robinson is pleased that through you, he is getting the better of your father. We mustn't disappoint him. I'll tell Geddes not to say anything, and I'll come back to the hotel and directly to your room; Robinson need never know. Now, give me those things and let me get on with it."

Reluctantly I handed over the clothes. I longed to go myself. I wanted to see Graham, wanted to have him grateful to me; but I believed Edith would have the better chance of carrying off Graham's escape. I told myself that was the important thing. Besides, I didn't like the idea of Robinson using me to get back at my father.

If I had any doubts, when I saw how cleverly Edith had draped the abeyah and veil, I felt sure of having made the right decision. Snatching up the carpetbag, she took the identity papers and steamer ticket. "I must go to my room to attend to a few things, and then I'll be off. You're to keep to your room, and remember, at all costs you're to stay away from Robinson."

The voice beneath the veil rattled off a string of Arabic words. I saw Edith would be a hundred times more effective than I would have been. For the first time, I felt encouraged. "Edith, I'm so grateful to you." But she was gone before I could finish thanking her.

I wanted to follow her to the ship, to be there when Graham escaped, but after Edith's warning I felt I had to stay out of the consul's way. I wondered if Saladin and the consul would be at the wharves, watching for me. They would see Arab women boarding the ship and not know which of the black-robed women might be me; certainly they would not guess one of them was Edith.

I passed the time by imagining Edith's journey from the hotel—how she would summon a carriage, travel through the crowded streets of Alexandretta, reach the wharves and dismiss her driver, and then make her way to the ship, walking up the gangplank past the guards, entering her cabin and opening the door that led to Graham.

There was a knock. Afraid it might be the consul, I didn't answer until I heard Hakki calling my name. I opened the door, and Hakki hurried into my room, a troubled expression on his face. "When it is so important for all of us to stay together, why does Miss Phillips depart without us?"

"I am sure she only went out for a short time. She'll be back directly."

"We are not sailing until tomorrow morning, but I just passed the porters on the stairs carrying off Miss Phillips's trunk and all the numerous things for her plants. Her room is empty and she is nowhere to be seen."

Fear, so slight as to be no more than the shadow of a rat's tail, brushed me. I asked Hakki, "Where could she be sending her things? I thought our luggage was not to be picked up until this evening."

"Exactly. So why is it her things go now and not by my arrangements?"

I grabbed Hakki's arm and forced him out into the hall and down the stairway. We reached the lobby as the carriage pulled away; it was loaded with Edith's luggage, all of which was thoroughly familiar to me. "You must ask the hotel porter where they are taking Edith's things," I ordered Hakki.

"To the *Poseidon*, sir," was the porter's answer. "There were very many boxes."

"Get me a carriage. Immediately," I told the man.

He was quick to sense my urgency and ran into the street. In a moment he was helping me into a carriage.

"But you mustn't go away as well," Hakki cried. "If you go, I must go with you, or you, too, will be lost."

As the carriage sped toward the wharf, my fear grew to suspicion and then to anger. It must have been Edith all along. I could hardly believe it, yet it made sense. With her knowledge of plants and her connivance with Mastur, who did the cooking and served us, Edith had managed to poison my father. When Father became ill and we had to stay behind, she arranged for Mohammed to remain with us, and then she sent her Metawileh thugs after him. My mind was racing. Of course it was Edith who turned in Monsieur Louvois and then Graham. When I'd told her about the consul's plan to rescue Graham, she had talked me into letting her take my place. Instead of rescuing Graham, she would see to it that he would be taken to Mersina and left to the mercy of the sultan's men. What I didn't understand was why she hated Father and Graham.

Hakki complained, "I don't know why you and the others hire me if you are always to go off on your own. What will Watson and Sons think of me if I have lost everyone?"

"Hakki, I know who complained to Watson and Sons. It was Edith."

His face crumpled. "How can that be? She said she would write in my favor. But if what you say is true, that is a cruel thing and I am not sorry she has gone her own way."

Remembering that Hakki had told us how he had once taught the children of the Turkish soldiers, I said, "Hakki, can't you do something for Graham? Couldn't you go to the Turkish authorities?"

A look of alarm spread over his face. "Miss Hamilton, you must know that I did not choose to be a tour leader. I loved my teaching. I am not a *hafiz*, a holy man who knows the Koran by heart and teaches in the traditional Islamic school where the students spend their days reciting aloud from the Holy Scriptures. As a child I attended such a school and grew to hate the boredom. I did not want to teach at such a school. My uncle Mehmet, who was in the Turkish army, pulled a few strings, and I found myself teaching at a military school.

"I was proud of my position and of my students, in their navy-blue uniforms decorated with rows of gold buttons and the star and crescent. Then one day I was called to the school and told that I would be excused from teaching the following term. I had been chosen to act as a tour director, yet not as a tour director. I was to understand that my position was highly secret. Alas, I was forced, against my will, to act as a spy for the Turkish government. No, no. I could not interfere with the authorities, as you call them."

By the time Hakki finished his story, we had reached the pier. The *Poseidon* was preparing to sail, and the pier was filled with the sad excitement of farewells. One passenger was carrying a freshly butchered lamb on board, another a tent made into a parcel. Dockworkers pitched bolts of silk and bundles of hides into the hold, along with burlap bags that emitted the sickly-sweet smell of licorice.

I saw how clever Robinson's plan had been, for the pier was crowded with Turks and Arabs. I could easily have slipped aboard in the crush of passengers hurrying onto the ship; instead, I had lost my nerve and given way to Edith. Hakki and I watched as the porters shouldered luggage up and down a gangplank that was guarded by a pair of Turkish soldiers. While I tried to think how I could possibly rescue Graham, two porters—an ancient man, much too old and decrepit for his burden, and a younger man who looked as though he might be the old man's son—struggled up the gangplank carrying Edith's trunk and specimen boxes and disappeared among the passengers milling about the deck.

Hakki pointed at them. "There, didn't I say?"

The pair reappeared and made their way down the gangplank. Waiting until the two porters were a safe distance from the ship, I ran up to them, pressing coins into the hand of the son. "To whom did you deliver that trunk just now?"

"To an English lady, Mademoiselle Phillips," he said.

"Not to an Arab lady?" I asked. "An Arab lady in an abeyah and veil?"

"An Arab lady with all that luggage? No, no, *effendim*. It went to the English lady whose name I gave to you."

"What destination was marked on them?"

"Istanbul, madam. She has also given to me a letter to deliver to the Hotel Tirsoni," he added, pleased to show his importance, "but for that I am to wait until the ship sails."

"For whom is the letter?"

"I don't know, *effendim*. I was to give it to the clerk in the hotel. The name is written down on the envelope, but English writing means nothing to me."

I looked at the envelope and read my name. "That is my name. You can give it to me."

"I was told to give it to the clerk at the hotel." The porter clearly wanted the pleasure of entering such a hotel.

"This is the lady named on the letter," Hakki confirmed. "Let her have it."

I handed the porter a gold sovereign. "Give it to me and it will save you the trouble of making the trip to the Tirsoni."

The father gave the son a greedy nudge, and the letter was handed over. A moment later the two men disappeared into the crowd.

I led Hakki to a café a short distance from the pier. Dockworkers, along with hangers-on who looked as though they made their living in secret ways, were gathered in sullen clumps around a handful of tables. They were clearly outraged that a woman should invade their café. I led a protesting Hakki to a back table and ordered coffee from a nervous waiter, not because I wanted the coffee but to get rid of the waiter, who was trying to find a polite way to ask us to leave. I tore open the envelope.

Dear Julia,

I have traveled among the Arabs for thirty years. They are my friends. I will not have interlopers come to their country to scavenge about for spoils. I have known from the beginning what all of you wanted. My "kidnapping" in Jerud was to give me an opportunity to inform the Arabs of your greedy errands. From Jerud the Metawilehs followed us about like good angels to do my bidding.

Your father came here to do the dirty work of England's Foreign Office, looking about to see what he could steal for the empire. It was a pleasure to watch this messenger of English lust grow weak and uncertain with my poison, a poison concocted from the plant of a country he would barter away and administered by Mastur, my friend and a loyal Arab. I am only sorry it did not do its job.

It was the same with Louvois, who crept about seeing where the French might move in as if this country were just another pretty trinket he might steal. I arranged for him to be allowed to keep his little collection of antiquities so that it would appear he was the one to betray Geddes, but be assured the customs officers will not be so generous, for they will be ready for him.

Hakki is nothing more than a spy sent to keep an eye on us for the Turks. I was pleased to denounce him to Watson & Sons so that he can no longer act the part of the informer; nor will the Turks be pleased with a spy who has failed.

By having Mastur delay the carriage while you and your father were in Ain el Beida, we were able to take care of Mohammed, who should not have betrayed his fellow Arabs by doing Geddes's work for him.

As for your friend Geddes, he thinks he is for the Arabs but he is for the Ottoman Empire. If Geddes's Young Turks are successful, they will forget the concessions they have promised to the Arabs—and the Greeks, Armenians, and Jews as well. The leaders of the Young Turks are, after all, Turks; and Turks will not be willing to preside at the dispersal of the Ottoman Empire. When the Arabs ask for the independence they have been promised by well-meaning fools like Geddes, do you believe for a moment the Young Turks will give it to them? The

Young Turks are more nationalistic than the sultan.
Geddes will die in Mersina, but he will not die quickly. I
made sure Professor Ladamacher, who wished to betray
the Arabs to the Germans, learned the same deadly lesson.

By the time you read this, the Poseidon will have
sailed. Put Geddes out of your mind. He cares nothing for
you; he is in love with his own ambition.

You ought to do something with your sketching: you
are really quite passable, and under other circumstances
we might have remained friends.

One day Turkey will be overthrown by the Arabs. It
is well known that in north Africa there are Arabs who
have kept hanging on their walls for four hundred years
the keys of houses in Spain's Seville and Granada, cities
that once were theirs.

As for me, I will ship my finds to the Royal Botanic
Gardens and then I will disappear into the desert. It is
where I belong and where I wish to die.

Edith

I clenched my fists to keep my hands from trembling and
turned my face aside so that the men in the café who were
staring at me should not see my tears of rage and frustration.
Graham would be taken off the boat at Mersina, and then

what? A Turkish prison? Torture? A firing squad? I recalled how close Mastur and Edith had been and how Mastur had always served Father first. She had meant Father to die.

"Miss Phillips says bad things?" Hakki put a consoling hand on my arm. "I think you had better return to the hotel and allow your father to give you help."

I let Hakki put me into a carriage, but against his protestations I refused to go back to the hotel. The moment I was alone, I called to the driver to ask him if he spoke English.

"Ah, and French and many German words. Today we are one country; tomorrow we may be another. It is well to be prepared."

"Can you take me to the the garrison?"

He gave my a wary look. "You have business with the soldiers?"

"Take me there," I commanded him, my voice so insistent that this time I had no need of giving baksheesh. He turned from me and signaled his horses. A moment before, he would have been my friend; now I had made of him a sullen servant, but I didn't care. My fear for Graham destroyed any last bit of patience I had.

I ordered the driver to leave me at the small, shabby administration building, where a slovenly orderly looked unsurprised by my request to see the commandant.

The orderly shrugged his shoulders and did not so much lead me as herd me into a small, dusty office almost entirely taken up by file boxes. An officer sat at a battered desk whose surface was dusted with cigarette ashes and decorated with rings from innumerable coffee cups. He held a pencil as if it were a weapon.

He rose to greet me, taking in my tumbled hair, my blouse half pulled from my skirt, the dusty shoes. "Mademoiselle," he said, bowing.

I blurted out, "You have an English subject under guard on the *Poseidon.* Surely you have no jurisdiction over him."

The man gave me a long look. "Everyone who comes to this country is under the Turkish law. If I were to come to your England, would I not have to follow the laws of England?"

"What do you mean to do with him?"

"You have an interest in this man? A relative, perhaps?"

"No, but he traveled with us. He is a friend."

"Ah," the man said. His tone made me blush. "What is it you would have me do?"

"Let him go. Whatever you are accusing him of, I am sure he meant no harm. All you have to go on is what Miss Phillips said, and she has a grudge against Graham Geddes."

The officer sipped at his coffee, watching me all the

while. "My superiors at Mersina already know of this Geddes," he said. "If the ship arrived there and he were not on it, they would would be angry and I would bear the brunt of that anger. If I did not give them your Mr. Geddes, I would have to give them something else." He had a look of hunger on his face. "Would you have something for me?"

I knew what I must do to save Graham—I must betray my father. I must say that a member of the British Foreign Office had been traveling incognito through Syria and was now here in Alexandretta. I must identify him as Carlton Hamilton and say he was in Turkey to find out what the Arab tribes think of Britain—whether they still trust Britain more than the French and the Turks. I must say Father hoped to make friends with the Arabs against the Turks. That was what I should say, but I could not speak the words. I could not betray Father, even for Graham.

Somehow I got out of the chair and stumbled from the room. The orderly gave me a bemused look. "Who will be the next English person?" he said, more to himself than to me.

"What do you mean?" I asked.

"First there was the British gentleman and now you come."

"What did the British gentleman look like?"

He described my father.

The officer had tried to trick me into identifying my father to add to what he already knew, and I had nearly given in to him. My father must have been there pleading for Graham.

The trip back to the hotel was the longest journey of my life. When at last I walked through the entrance, I saw Graham standing at the lobby desk, his luggage like small friendly creatures nestled about his long legs. He was without a hat, and his hair was rumpled. Somewhere along the way he had lost his tie and jacket. He appeared shrunken, and his tan had faded to a jaundiced yellow. I stood there for a long minute, afraid to approach him lest he turn out to be some sort of phantom who would disappear when I reached out for him.

The presence of the clerk, ostentatiously shuffling papers while secretly watching us, made my greeting of Graham awkward, so instead of showing how relieved I was to see him, I could only clasp his hand and hang on to it. His lack of response made even my slight show of affection seem overwrought.

"Have they let you go?" The evidence was there before my eyes, but I wanted to hear it from Graham.

"As you see," he said, "thanks to your father. I must say

I didn't expect help from that quarter."

Much to the disappointment of the clerk Graham moved away from the desk, directing me to a corner of the lobby. I sank down on a couch and waited for him sit down next to me. Instead, he continued standing, so that in order to avoid the awkwardness of distance, I had to get up again. I saw that he was in a hurry.

"Edith had thought to have me all dried and pressed like one of her posies," he said. "As soon as she opened the door to my cabin and I had a look at the pleased expression on her face, like a cat with a bowl of cream, I guessed she was behind all our trouble. But you should have seen her expression change when the Turks escorted me off the boat. That woman is capable of murder." There was something like admiration in his voice.

I asked "What do you mean 'thanks to my father'?"

"Your father got on to the Foreign Office by wire and London suggested to the Turks that there might be a diplomatic dustup if they didn't let loose of me. Your father then went to the Turkish officers who had arrested me and demanded my release. I'm afraid that will mean trouble for your father back home with the Foreign Office."

My world was turning upside down. It was father who

had saved Graham. I could only guess what he had sacrificed to do it.

"Your father's superiors—though indeed they are not—will be unhappy with having to waste some of their influence with the sultan on a creature as trivial as I am, and not only trivial, but a nuisance for England, for your father knows perfectly well I have no intention of giving up my fight for the Young Turks. I'm afraid I underestimated your father; he's been rather good to me."

Thinking of my near betrayal of Father, I felt sick. Because I cared for Graham, my father had risked his career to save him. "What will you do now?" I had seen Graham's luggage.

He lowered his voice. "I don't suppose the Turks are anxious to have me underfoot in Syria. I'm going to attempt to get into the Jebel Druze, which is the homeland of my Druze tribes. I'm going by steamer to Haifa, and I'll try to make my way overland by way of Jerusalem. Once in the Jebel Druze, I'll know how to lose myself. I think I can promise you next year at this time the sultan will be doing what the Young Turks tell him."

I had been waiting for some mention of myself in his plans. Now, trying to make it sound like a pleasantry, I said, "Will I see you again?"

"Your father's been awfully decent to me."

"Was promising not to see me a condition of your release?"

"Certainly not. But I know your father doesn't approve of my way of life, and I'm not about to change. He does not want you involved with me."

I had had enough of people believing they knew what was best for me. "Why should it be you or my father who feels he must decide things for me?"

Graham looked around, embarrassed at my outburst. "I'm afraid I've made trouble for you, Julia. The truth is I'm not very good with people one by one. I do better with causes, but I don't apologize for that. If there weren't men of my kind, where would the world be? If you take people one by one, they're seldom worth fighting for."

"That's a terrible thing to say. How can you be so cynical? If that's how you feel, why should you think any better of a mass of people?"

"All the individual nastiness gets hidden in the crowd." His voice took on the angry intensity I had heard before. "Don't think because he got me out of a Turkish jail I don't still oppose your father."

I thought my father was right to say romanticism leads to disappointment. "I am sorry for you," I said. I was glad to leave him.

I found my father in his room. He was sitting in a chair doing nothing. This inactivity, so unlike him, was unsettling. I saw he was sitting there waiting for me. To have all his attention was intimidating. I had practiced my confession, but faced with his quiet watchfulness I could only blurt out, "I nearly told the officer at the garrison what you were doing in Syria."

"Ah, but you didn't. However, I am now persona non grata in this counntry. The Turks are anxious to have me out of here. They'll keep an eye on me until we sail tomorrow. The Turkish Foreign Office will have got on to the British Foreign Office by now to protest my being here. However, that doesn't matter, for I have already sent my resignation in to the Foreign Office."

"What do you mean?"

"When we talked last night, you seemed very keen on getting Geddes away from the Turks. I wired the Foreign Office this morning, and they established a liaison with the Turkish government. By the time I went to the officer in charge of the garrison, everything had been worked out. Geddes must have been released at about the same time you were on your way to the garrison. Of course I had no idea you would go to the Turkish army with the thought of turning me in." Father looked at me with something between dismay and admiration, as if I were a child who has displayed some outrageous behavior that is both loathsome and interesting.

"Why didn't the officer tell me that you had already spoken to him and that Graham was being released?"

"He must have believed letting you think otherwise might get him useful information."

I flushed. "But it didn't."

"I'm glad of that."

"Why must you resign?"

"Without badly compromising my principles, I could hardly ask the British Foreign Office to go to great lengths to release a man who was bound to do England nothing but mischief."

"Did you make Graham so grateful for your help, he would agree not to see me again?"

"There was no request and no agreement."

"But you guessed at what he would do."

"I knew what he would do."

"You may be pleased to hear that I am altogether disappointed in him."

"You are surprised by Geddes's priorities; I am not, but I am sorry someone for whom you cared has disappointed you. Graham will go elsewhere and create another muddle out of the best will in the world, and someone will have to mop up after him just as I did here. Whatever you may think now, you will eventually see I acted in your best interests."

"Why didn't you just let him be carried off by the Turks?"

"He would have remained forever a martyr in your eyes, a romantic figure against whom you would measure the commonplace men of the world. At least this way you have seen Geddes for what he is."

I smiled. "I'm not sure I should I thank you for that."

"I didn't do it for your thanks. To tell you the truth, I was getting to rather like Geddes. It is not all bad to have impossible dreams when you are his age. Certainly there will be no time for them later."

I showed Father Edith's letter. He read it slowly, as though it were in some obscure language.

"The woman is mad," he said. "We'll send the letter on to the authorities, of course, but I don't suppose they will give it much notice. Anyhow, I expect Edith will soon be on her way to some distant Bedouin encampment." He looked at the letter again, and a smile played about his lips. "She might have killed me." He was enjoying a little rush of excitement.

"Where will we go now?" I asked.

"Wherever we like," he said. "I am sure with your romantic tendencies it is only a matter of time before you find another chap like Geddes. I may as well enjoy your company while I can."

"I've always wanted to see the pyramids."

"Then you shall," he promised. "You will find Egypt a country full of surprises."

EPILOGUE

*I*N 1909, TWO YEARS after this story takes place, the Young Turks compelled Sultan Abdülhamid II to reinstate the Turkish Constitution of 1876. One of the leaders of the Young Turks, Envar Bey, said, "We are all brothers. There are no longer Bulgars, Greeks, Roumanians, Jews, Mussulmans [Muslims]; under the same blue sky we are all equal, we glory in being Ottomans."

Shortly thereafter, the Ottoman Empire began to fall apart. Austria advanced on Bosnia and Herzegovina. Greece took Crete. Albania declared its independence. Italian troops landed in Tripoli. The Kurds and Yemenis and the Armenians rose up, as did the Arab countries.

The Young Turks, seeing their Ottoman lands dwindle, began to tighten the reins of empire in an effort to choke the nationalistic forces they had let loose. They became more oppressive than the sultan had been, punishing any group wishing its independence.

During World War I, Britain, Italy, France, and Russia met secretly to divide the Ottoman Empire among themselves. France took over Syria, dividing it into six parts. The French language became compulsory in the schools, where students of all nationalities were required to sing the French national anthem, "La Marseillaise."